PRIDE AND PREJUDICE AND WITCHES

A SHORT BEWITCHING, SPICY, REGENCY, ENEMIES TO LOVERS, ROMANCE

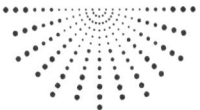

JAX WILDER

Pride and Prejudice and Witches© 2024 by Jax Wilder

Published by Rainbow Quartz Publishing

RQPublishing.com

RainbowQuartzPublishing@gmail.com

Edmonds, WA 98026

ISBN: 978-1-961714-48-9

Cover design by Miranda Townsend

Edited by Miranda Townsend

First Edition: September, 2024

For the peeps who make Pride and Prejudice memes. They are my jam.

Jax Wilder

ELIZABETH

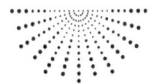

*I*t is a truth universally acknowledged that a witch, in possession of a good set of charms, must be in want of a cup of tea-or, at least, that's how I felt after spending an entire evening hunched over the workbench in my family's magical shop, Bennet's Charms & Curiosities. My fingers were sore from threading protective stones onto delicate chains, and the scent of lavender and sage clung to my hair like a stubborn spell. The shop was alive with the soft hum of residual magic, the enchanted trinkets and potions casting a faint, comforting glow in the dim light.

"Lizzie, darling, are you still at it?" My mother's voice floated in from the shop's front room, where she was likely reorganizing the crystal display for the third time that day. The air around her was always tinged with a subtle magical aura, a mix of her own energy and the residual spells she constantly cast to keep the shop running smoothly.

"I'm nearly done!" I called back, carefully knotting the last charm with a bit more force than necessary. "Just finishing up this batch for Mrs. Long. She wanted extra protection for her herb garden—something about a neighbor's cat and suspicious claw marks."

"Cats," my mother sniffed, appearing in the doorway with her usual air of mild disapproval. She waved her hand, and the crystals behind her flickered, rearranging themselves into a more aesthetically pleasing pattern. "Always meddling with things they shouldn't. You'd think they'd have better manners, being so close to witches all the time."

I grinned as I slid the last charm into a velvet pouch and sealed it with a flick of my wrist, the knot tightening itself with a faint spark of magic. Every witch's power is different. Mine is tied to charms and spells, while others, like Jane, can heal with just a touch. But we all have our limits. Too much magic in one day, and the energy will drain us. "Well, we can't all be well-mannered witches, can we?"

"Indeed not." She gave me a look that was both

indulgent and exasperated—something she had perfected over the years. A faint shimmer of magic danced around her fingertips as she adjusted the position of a stray crystal on a nearby shelf. "Speaking of which, where are your sisters? It's not like them to leave you to do all the work."

"Oh, you know Jane," I said, stretching my arms above my head and feeling a satisfying crack in my spine. A small puff of magic escaped my fingers, twinkling like stardust before dissipating into the air. "She's probably lost in a book of healing spells or dreaming up new ways to make the perfect love potion. And Lydia—well, I imagine she's somewhere causing trouble, as usual."

"Typical," my mother sighed, though there was a fondness in her voice that belied the complaint. "I swear, if Lydia doesn't find a respectable suitor soon, I don't know what we'll do with her." She snapped her fingers, and a broom swept across the floor, tidying up the remnants of the day's work.

That was my mother in a nutshell: always thinking about the future and, more specifically, our futures. My sisters and I had long since accepted that Mrs. Bennet's primary mission in life was to see all of us married off to suitable partners—preferably ones with strong magical bloodlines and deep pockets.

I stood up and dusted off my hands, feeling a sense of satisfaction that only comes from a job well done. The protective charms glowed softly in their pouches, a testament to the care I had put into crafting them. "Well, if any suitor can handle Lydia, they'll be the strongest warlock in the land."

Mother smiled, but her eyes were already drifting toward the front window, where the last rays of the setting sun cast long shadows across the shop's wooden floor. A gentle breeze, carrying a faint trace of magic, stirred the air around us. "Speaking of suitors, did you hear the news, Lizzie?"

I raised an eyebrow, intrigued by the shift in her tone. "What news?"

"The Bingleys have arrived at Netherfield Hall," she announced, her voice practically buzzing with excitement. A flick of her wrist sent a cascade of light through the shop, illuminating the crystals with an ethereal glow. "I heard it from Mrs. Lucas just this afternoon. They're a wealthy family—practically mundanes in their abilities, mind you, but well-connected. And, more importantly, they've brought a friend with them. A Mr. Darcy."

"Darcy," I repeated, rolling the name around in

my mind as if testing a new flavor of potion. A faint tingle of anticipation ran through my fingers, sparking a small, harmless arc of magic. "And what's so special about this Mr. Darcy?"

My mother leaned in conspiratorially, her eyes sparkling with the thrill of gossip. "He's a sorcerer, Lizzie. And not just any sorcerer—a powerful one, from what I hear. Comes from one of the oldest magical families in England."

I couldn't help but smile at her enthusiasm. My mother lived for moments like this—whispers of new arrivals, tales of eligible bachelors with mysterious backgrounds, and the endless possibilities they presented for her daughters. "Let me guess," I said, trying to keep my tone light, "you're already planning how to introduce us."

"Well," she said with a sly grin, "it wouldn't hurt to make a good impression. A sorcerer of his stature... he could be just the match for you, Lizzie."

"Oh, Mother," I laughed, shaking my head. A soft, warm light glowed from the enchanted lanterns above, casting playful shadows that danced along the walls. "You know I'm not interested in that sort of thing. I'm perfectly happy here in the shop, brewing potions and making charms."

But even as I said it, I felt a flicker of curiosity. A

powerful sorcerer in Longbourn Hollow? It wasn't every day that someone like that came to our sleepy little town. And if I was being honest, part of me was intrigued—not by the idea of marriage, but by the challenge of meeting someone who might actually be worth my time.

"Just promise me you'll keep an open mind," my mother said, reaching out to straighten a strand of my hair that had escaped its loose braid. Her touch was gentle, infused with a warmth that only a mother's magic could bring. "You never know where life will take you, Lizzie."

I smiled and leaned into her touch, appreciating the rare moment of quiet between us. The air around us seemed to hum with potential, the magic in the shop responding to our thoughts and emotions. "I promise," I said, though in my heart, I was certain that no sorcerer—no matter how powerful—could distract me from the life I had built here in Longbourn Hollow.

But as I locked up the shop and stepped out into the cool evening air, the gentle breeze carried the faint scent of jasmine and magic, swirling around me like a whispered secret. I couldn't help but wonder what this Mr. Darcy might be like. After all,

magic had a way of surprising even the most stubborn of witches, and I was nothing if not stubborn.

2
DARCY

he air in Longbourn Hollow was thick with the scent of earth and old magic, the kind that clung to the bones of the place and settled into the very stones of the houses. As the enchanted carriage rolled up the gravel drive of Netherfield Hall, I couldn't help but feel a sense of unease prickling at the back of my neck. This town, with its quaint cottages and winding lanes, was a far cry from the grand estates and sophisticated circles I was accustomed to.

"Isn't it charming, Darcy?" Charles Bingley, seated beside me, leaned forward to catch a better view of the sprawling grounds. His enthusiasm was almost infectious, but I kept my expression carefully neutral. The magical wards around the carriage shimmered faintly, a subtle reminder of the protection spells woven into the very fabric of our lives.

"Charming," I echoed, though my tone lacked the warmth of his. I could appreciate the Hall's historic architecture, the way the ivy climbed up the weathered stone walls, twisting with an almost sentient intent, but there was something about this place that felt... rustic. And not in a way that appealed to me. The old magic here was thick, untamed, and it hummed just beneath the surface, like a slumbering beast waiting to be awakened.

"Louisa and Caroline are already enamored," Charles continued, oblivious to my lack of enthusiasm. "They've been talking about redecorating since we passed the town limits. Imagine what they'll do to the ballroom."

I managed a polite nod, but my thoughts were elsewhere. It wasn't just the town's lack of refinement that troubled me—though that was certainly a factor—it was the undercurrent of magic that thrummed through the air, old and wild. Longbourn Hollow had a reputation for being a place where the lines between the magical and mundane blurred, where the old ways still held sway over the modern.

It was precisely the kind of place I had been taught to approach with caution.

As we stepped out of the carriage, I took in the surroundings with a critical eye. The house itself was stately enough for some, though it bore the marks of age and the whisper of ancient spells woven into its foundations. The gardens, once manicured and precise, had grown wild around the edges, as if the very earth was resisting the control of the humans who tended it. I could feel the pull of the land, the magic in the soil, strong and unyielding.

"Darcy, you're frowning again," Bingley chided lightly, clapping me on the shoulder. A soft ripple of magic spread from his touch, an unintentional manifestation of his excitement. "I thought you might enjoy the change of scenery."

"I'm simply adjusting," I replied, smoothing the frown from my face as best I could. The magic in this place was different—unrefined, potent, and unpredictable. "This town... it's different from what I expected."

"Different can be good," he said, ever the optimist. "I think you'll come to appreciate it here. The people seem friendly, and I've heard there's a strong magical community."

"That's precisely what concerns me," I muttered, but Charles had already bounded up the steps to greet his sisters, who were inspecting the entrance hall with a mixture of delight and disdain.

As we entered the house, the sense of unease grew. The magic here was palpable, woven into the very fabric of the building. It was old magic, the kind that didn't conform to the rules of modern society, and I could feel it pressing in on me from all sides. The walls seemed to hum with energy, ancient spells etched into the stonework, their power thrumming faintly beneath my fingertips as I passed.

I forced myself to focus on the practicalities, directing the staff to where our belongings should be taken, ensuring that the wards around the house were strong enough to keep out any unwanted magical intrusions. This was, after all, a town where such precautions were necessary. The air around us was thick with the whispers of forgotten incantations, and I reinforced the protective spells with a murmured word, feeling the wards settle more firmly into place.

But even as I busied myself with these tasks, my mind drifted back to the encounter I'd had just a week before, with George Wickham. His smirk, the way he'd casually tossed about thinly veiled threats as if they were mere trifles, still grated on me. Wickham was a warlock of no small talent, but his moral compass had always been lacking. And now, it seemed, he had a new scheme in the works—one that undoubtedly involved me.

"Darcy, do come look at this," Caroline called from the drawing room, her voice carrying that air of imperiousness she so often employed. The chandelier above her head glowed with a soft, enchanted light, casting shimmering patterns across the walls.

Reluctantly, I joined them, offering a cursory glance at the ornate fireplace she was admiring. The hearthstones were etched with ancient runes, their meanings lost to time but still potent with latent magic. But my thoughts were still on Wickham, and on the letter I had received shortly after our encounter, delivered by a raven that bore Lady Catherine's seal.

The letter had been brief, as her correspondence often was, but its message was clear:

Be cautious. Longbourn Hollow is not the place for our kind. The Bennet family, in particular, is of particular distane. Remember your duty, Fitzwilliam—protect the family's magical heritage. Do not allow yourself to be distracted by lesser witches.

Lesser witches. I could almost hear the disdain dripping from her voice as I read the words. My aunt's obsession with maintaining the purity of our bloodline was as unyielding as ever, and while I understood the importance of upholding our magical traditions, her rigid views often felt stifling. The old blood demanded strict adherence to tradition, and Lady Catherine was its most fervent guardian.

Lady Catherine's words echoed. "Remember your duty, Fitzwilliam." It wasn't just about bloodlines. It was about protecting the power my family had built over centuries—power that was slipping through my fingers.

Still, there was truth in her warning. This town, with its old magic and hidden secrets, was a far cry from the controlled, regulated environment of our family estates. It was a place where power could shift unexpectedly, where alliances were not always what they seemed. The air itself seemed to pulse with possibilities, the future unfurling like the tendrils of ivy that crept up the walls of Netherfield Hall.

And yet, as I stood there in the drawing room, listening to Caroline and Louisa debate the merits of velvet versus silk drapery, I couldn't shake the feeling that this place had more to offer than I had initially thought. The magic here was raw, untamed, and though it made me uneasy, it also intrigued me. There was something about the unpredictability of it, the way it refused to be tamed, that stirred a long-buried sense of challenge within me.

Perhaps Bingley was right—different could be good. But I would remain vigilant. In a town like Longbourn Hollow, one could never be too careful. The very air seemed to whisper secrets, and I had no intention of being caught unawares.

And as for this Bennet family... I would reserve judgment until I had the opportunity to observe them myself. After all, a sorcerer's duty was to protect—not just his own, but those who could not protect themselves. And if Lady Catherine's warning was anything to go by, the Bennets might require more protection than they realized.

The sun began to set, casting long shadows across the grounds of Netherfield Hall, and I felt the old magic of the town settle around me like a mantle. This place, with its secrets and its power, was unlike any I had known before. And as much as it unsettled me, I could not deny that it also called to me, beckoning me to uncover the mysteries that lay hidden beneath its surface.

3

ELIZABETH

he air was alive with the buzz of chatter and the crackle of magic as we entered the grand hall of the Longbourn Hollow Community Center. Every year, the local magical gathering was the event of the season—an opportunity for witches, warlocks, and all manner of magical beings to mingle, swap spells, and maybe even show off a bit. This year, however, there was an extra charge in the atmosphere, something electric that set my nerves tingling like the spark before a spell.

"Elizabeth, do fix your hair," my mother fussed as we stepped through the door, her eyes already scanning the room for eligible bachelors—or rather, their magical potential. The faint glow of her own aura shimmered around her, a subtle but constant reminder of the magic that flowed through our veins. "And Jane, darling, you look positively radiant. I'm sure you'll catch someone's eye tonight."

Jane, ever the picture of grace, smiled softly and tucked a loose strand of her blonde hair behind her ear. A soft shimmer of magic trailed her fingers, subtly enhancing her already ethereal beauty. "Thank you, Mama."

I rolled my eyes affectionately at Jane as I straightened my own curls, which had decided to frizz out in defiance of all charms. No matter how many times I cast a smoothing spell, my hair seemed to have a mind of its own. "Mama, we're here to enjoy ourselves, remember? Not just to—"

"To make a good impression," she interrupted, her gaze fixing on a group of well-dressed men across the room. "And that, my dear Lizzie, is precisely what I intend for all of you to do."

I sighed but couldn't help the small smile that tugged at my lips. My mother might have been single-minded in her pursuit of husbands for her daughters, but her heart was in the right place. Besides, I was curious about this gathering. The arrival of the Bingleys—and their mysterious sorcerer friend—had everyone talking, and I wasn't immune to a bit of intrigue myself.

The room was a sea of familiar faces, interspersed with a few new ones. Old Mrs. Long was holding court near the refreshment table, animatedly discussing the benefits of batwing potions with Mr. Phillips. A group of young witches were showing off their new wands, each one glowing with the soft light of freshly cast enchantments, sparks flying as they giggled and flirted with a pair of warlocks. The air was thick with the scent of brewing potions, burning incense, and the faint ozone tang of active spells.

And then, I saw them.

Charles Bingley was instantly recognizable, standing near the center of the room with an easy smile and a warm laugh that made me think of sun-dappled meadows and open skies. There was a gentle, almost soothing magic that radiated from him, enveloping those around him in a comforting aura. Beside him stood his sisters, Louisa and Caroline, dressed to the nines in enchanted gowns that shimmered like water in moonlight, surveying the room with an air of detached amusement. Their magical auras were sharp, polished, and carefully controlled, as if they were aware of every eye upon them.

But it was the man standing just behind them

who caught my attention—tall, dark-haired, with an expression as unreadable as stone. Fitzwilliam Darcy. Even from across the room, I could feel the power radiating off him, like a fire burning just beneath the surface, restrained but ever-present. His aura was different from the others—dark and potent, coiled tightly around him as if held in check by sheer force of will. It was the kind of magic that demanded respect, even fear.

I straightened unconsciously, my eyes narrowing as I studied him. He was handsome, yes, but there was something else, something that made me bristle. An air of superiority, perhaps, that set him apart from the rest of us. He carried himself with a certain arrogance, as if he were above the gathering, above all of us. His aura was as controlled as his expression, the power within it carefully concealed, yet unmistakably formidable.

But despite myself, I couldn't help but be intrigued. It wasn't often that someone with such raw magical power crossed my path, and I found myself wanting to know more about this enigmatic sorcerer, even as I sensed he was not the type to lower himself to small talk.

I was so absorbed in my observations that I didn't notice Jane slipping away until I turned and found her missing. Scanning the room, I spotted her near the refreshment table, where Charles Bingley had just approached her, his smile widening as they exchanged pleasantries. Their auras mingled briefly, a soft intertwining of warmth and light that made me smile. There was an easy, natural connection between them, the kind that was rare and precious.

"Mama's going to be pleased," I muttered under my breath, watching as Jane and Bingley struck up a conversation. There was an easy warmth between them, the kind that was natural and unforced. Jane's soft laugh floated across the room, and I couldn't help but smile. If anyone deserved to find happiness, it was Jane.

As I turned back toward the center of the room. Darcy's gaze was fixed on me, dark and intense, like a predator sizing up its prey. My breath caught in my throat when I noticed there was something predatory in the way he looked at me. His eyes roamed over my body with a deliberate slowness that left me feeling exposed, as though he were undressing me right there, stripping me down layer by layer. His expression was inscrutable, but there was a flicker of something in those stormy eyes— curiosity, yes, but something else too, something darker and far more dangerous.

My skin prickled under his gaze, a wave of heat washing over me, pooling low in my belly. His aura flared slightly, a ripple of energy that brushed against me like a caress, sending a shiver down my spine. It was as if the very air around us had thickened, charged with an almost unbearable tension. I lifted my chin, refusing to be cowed by the power that radiated from him, but even as I did, I felt a dangerous thrill at the way he looked at me, like he could see through my clothes, through my defenses, straight to the raw desire simmering beneath the surface.

But then, with infuriating casualness, he looked away, dismissing me as if I were of no consequence at all. The sting of his disregard burned hotter than I cared to admit, a sharp pang of frustration and wounded pride. How dare he look at me like that, only to cast me aside as if I were nothing? I clenched my fists, my nails biting into my palms as I fought to maintain my composure.

"Well then," I thought, my anger simmering just beneath the surface, fueled by the potent mix of desire and indignation swirling within me. It was one thing to be intrigued by someone so powerful, but quite another to be so casually dismissed by them. The nerve of him.

I moved toward the refreshment table, but his presence was impossible to ignore, a constant, oppressive weight pressing down on me, heightening my awareness of him until it was almost unbearable. His dark aura seemed to coil around me, pulling me into his orbit, even as I tried to resist the pull. The air was thick with the scent of him, rich and intoxicating, and I couldn't help but feel a flicker of irritation at his apparent indifference. But that irritation only deepened the ache in my core, an ache that I couldn't simply will away.

Then, suddenly, his deep voice cut through the fog of my thoughts. "Miss Bennet," he said, and I turned to find him standing beside me, close enough that I could feel the heat radiating off his body. The air between us sizzled with tension, and I had to fight the urge to step even closer, to press myself against him and lose myself in the storm that raged just beneath his cool exterior.

"I see you are well acquainted with the local community," he said, his tone deceptively polite, but his eyes betrayed him. They were dark and hungry, smoldering with an intensity that made my breath hitch.

"Indeed, Mr. Darcy," I replied, my voice steadier than I felt. The thrum of desire in my veins made it difficult to think, let alone speak. "I find it important to engage with those around me."

His gaze lingered on me, and I could feel it, hot and heavy, like a physical touch. My pulse quickened, my heart pounding so loudly I was certain he could hear it. "Engagement is one thing, Miss Bennet. Mastery is another," he said, his voice low and rough, sending a shiver of anticipation through me. "I've noticed your magic—strong, but unrefined. It would benefit from a more disciplined approach."

The condescension in his tone was unmistakable, and it stoked the flames of my anger. But even as I bristled at his words, I couldn't deny the way my body responded to the authority in his voice, to the promise of what he could teach me, of how he could push me, bend me, shape me into something even more powerful. I wasn't sure if I wanted to slap him or throw myself at him and tear his clothes off.

"Unrefined?" I repeated, my voice laced with disbelief, but there was an undercurrent of something else too—desire, barely contained, bubbling just beneath the surface. "I wasn't aware that my magic required your approval, Mr. Darcy."

His eyes narrowed slightly, his aura pulsing with a subtle but unmistakable tension that resonated deep within me. "I only meant to suggest that with proper guidance, you could harness your abilities more effectively. There is a certain... power in restraint, Miss Bennet. One that you may not fully appreciate."

His words were maddeningly calm, and yet, they sent a thrill of heat through me, pooling low in my belly. There was a challenge in his tone, a dare that made my breath quicken, my body aching with the need to prove him wrong, to show him just how powerful my passion could be. "Restraint, Mr. Darcy, may be your preferred method," I replied, my voice barely above a whisper, "but I find that passion and instinct have their own value. Perhaps we simply have different approaches to magic."

His gaze bore into me, and for a moment, I could see it in his eyes—the desire, the hunger that mirrored my own. "Indeed, it seems we do," he said, his voice dropping to a husky murmur that sent a shiver down my spine. "But be careful, Miss Bennet. Passion, unchecked, can lead to recklessness."

The implication was clear, and it stung more than I cared to admit. But rather than let him see how much his words had affected me, I met his gaze head-on, defiant, even as my body trembled with the desire to close the distance between us, to press myself against him and feel the full force of the power that crackled between us. "And restraint, Mr. Darcy, can lead to stagnation," I shot back, my voice low and breathy. "It is through passion that we grow, that we push the boundaries of what we believe possible."

He studied me for a long moment, his expression unreadable, but I could feel the tension between us, thick and palpable, like a live wire ready to snap. "Perhaps you are right," he conceded, his voice soft, almost intimate. "But I would caution you to balance your passion with wisdom. Magic is a powerful force, and it should be wielded with care."

I forced a smile, though the tension between us was nearly suffocating. "Thank you for your advice, Mr. Darcy," I said, my voice strained with the effort it took to remain composed. "I shall consider it carefully."

With that, I turned on my heel and walked away, my heart pounding with a mixture of anger and frustration. But even as I moved away from him, I could still feel his gaze on me, hot and hungry, like a brand against my skin. How dare he criticize my magic, my approach to the very thing that defined who I was? Yet, as much as I hated to admit it, his words had struck a chord. Was there truth in what he said? Was I too reckless, too passionate in my magic?

No, I told myself firmly, trying to ignore the lingering heat between my legs. Darcy might be powerful, but he was not infallible. I would continue to trust in my instincts, in the passion that had always guided me. And I would prove, not just to him but to myself, that my approach was just as valid, just as strong as his.

But even as I walked away, I couldn't shake the feeling that this was far from over. The tension between us was like a spark, ready to ignite at any moment, and I knew that the next time we crossed paths, the flames would only burn hotter.

As I moved to rejoin Jane and Bingley, the tension from my encounter with Darcy still crackled in the air around me, like the lingering scent of smoke after a fire. My heart was still pounding, my thoughts swirling with the intensity of our exchange. I couldn't shake the feeling that this was only the beginning of my conflict with Darcy—that the sparks that had flown between us were just the first flickers of a much larger blaze.

We were two sides of the same coin, both powerful in our own ways, but fundamentally different in our views on magic and life. Where he saw control, I saw freedom; where he valued restraint, I cherished passion. It was more than just a difference of opinion—it was a clash of ideologies, a battle between two forces that could not coexist peacefully. And something deep inside me told me that our paths were destined to cross again, in ways I could not yet foresee.

But one thing was certain: I would not back down. Not now, not ever. The fire that burned within me would not be extinguished by Darcy's cold logic or his maddening calm. If anything, his arrogance had only stoked the flames, fueling my determination to prove that my way—my passion, my instinct—was just as valid, just as powerful, as his carefully controlled magic.

As I reached Jane and Bingley, I forced a smile, but the tension still thrummed beneath my skin, a constant reminder of the battle that had just begun. Darcy might think he could intimidate me, might believe that his power could overshadow mine, but he was wrong. The storm that had been brewing between us was only gathering strength, and I was more than ready to face it head-on.

Our paths would cross again—of that, I was certain. And when they did, I would be ready. Ready to stand my ground, to meet his power with my own, and to show him that there was more to magic than control and restraint. There was passion, and fire, and the wild, untamed force that lived within me. And I would prove, to him and to myself, that I was not someone to be dismissed or underestimated.

This was only the beginning. The next time our worlds collided, the sparks would fly even hotter, and I would be prepared to face whatever came next. Because I knew, deep in my soul, that I was just as strong as Darcy—if not stronger. And I would not let him—or anyone—diminish the power that burned within me.

4

ELIZABETH

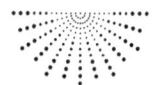

*B*ack at Bennet's Charms & Curiosities, the warm, familiar scent of herbs and potions wrapped around me like a comforting cloak. The shop, with its shelves brimming with enchanted trinkets and magical supplies, was a sanctuary—a place where I could escape the complexities of social gatherings and the enigmatic figures they often attracted.

Jane was organizing a display of crystal amulets, her delicate hands moving with practiced grace. The soft glow of the crystals reflected in her eyes, making her look as if she were lost in a pleasant daydream. "The Longbourn Hollow Ball was enchanting, wasn't it?" she said, her voice soft and dreamlike, a smile curving her lips. "Charles

Bingley is quite the gentleman, and his magical aura is so gentle and warm. I could talk to him for hours."

Lydia, ever impatient, rolled her eyes but couldn't hide her curiosity. "What did you two talk about, Jane? Was it all just polite nonsense, or did he actually say something interesting?"

Jane's smile deepened, and she sighed softly, her hands pausing for a moment as she recalled the evening. "Oh, it was so much more than polite conversation, Lydia. We talked about everything— magic, books, life... He's so well-read, so thoughtful. He has this way of looking at the world that's both refreshing and comforting."

I leaned in, unable to resist Jane's enthusiasm. "Books, you say? What kind? Did he have any favorites?"

Jane's eyes lit up, and she nodded eagerly. "He mentioned that he loves ancient magical texts— especially ones that explore the origins of enchantments and spells. We spent nearly an hour discussing one of his favorites, *The Arcane Histories*. He's fascinated by the way magic has evolved over the centuries, how it's shaped societies and even our understanding of morality."

Lydia snorted softly, but there was a glint of

interest in her eyes. "So, he's well read then? I suppose that's a good thing."

Jane laughed lightly, her fingers trailing over the delicate chains of the amulets. "He is, but in the most charming way. He's not just knowledgeable—he's passionate about learning. And it's not just books, either. We talked about life, too. He asked me what I thought about using magic in everyday tasks, how it could enhance or even complicate our lives."

"Did he now?" I asked, intrigued. "And what did you tell him?"

Jane's cheeks flushed a delicate pink as she recounted the conversation. "I told him that while magic is a gift, it's important to use it with intention. That sometimes, the simplest things in life—like baking a loaf of bread or tending to a garden—are more fulfilling when done by hand, without spells. He agreed and said that there's something pure about engaging with the world without relying on magic for everything."

Lydia leaned back, crossing her arms. "It sounds a bit boring, doesn't it? But what about the fun stuff? Did he show you any fancy spells?"

Jane's smile turned mischievous. "He did, actually. Just a small one—he conjured a bouquet of flowers from thin air, right in the middle of our conversation. It was so effortless, and the flowers were enchanted to change colors depending on my mood. It was the sweetest gesture."

I couldn't help but smile at the image of Jane, holding a bouquet that reflected her emotions, glowing softly in the candlelight. "He sounds like quite the catch, Jane. It's no wonder you're so taken with him."

Jane's expression grew more thoughtful, her fingers absently tracing the edge of a crystal pendant. "It's more than that, Lizzy. There's a kindness in him, a genuine warmth that's so rare. He listens—really listens—and he's so interested in what others have to say. It's not just that he's charming or well-mannered; it's that he's... good. I can't explain it, but I feel like I've known him for much longer than just a few days. Like there's this connection between us, something deep and meaningful."

Lydia groaned, but there was a teasing glint in her eyes. "You've got it bad, Jane. Next, you'll be telling us he's already proposed!"

Jane blushed even more, shaking her head. "Nothing like that, of course. But... well, I wouldn't be opposed to seeing where things might lead."

I watched Jane carefully, noting the way her eyes sparkled when she talked about Bingley. There was something in her tone, a quiet certainty that was so unlike the usual light-hearted infatuations one might expect at such gatherings. She was truly smitten, and for good reason, it seemed.

Lydia, perched on the edge of the counter, swung her legs idly. "And what about George Wickham? He's absolutely charming! We spent some time chatting, and he's got this way about him that just makes you want to smile."

I paused, my fingers trailing over a collection of spell books. There was something about Wickham that had nagged at me. His charm was undeniable, but there was a slickness to it, a calculated effort to endear himself to everyone. "Lydia, be careful with Wickham. I can't put my finger on it, but there's something more going on with him. Something I don't quite trust."

Lydia waved off my concern with a light laugh. "Oh, Lizzy, you worry too much! Wickham's just being friendly. Besides, you have bigger things to think about—like Mr. Darcy."

My stomach fluttered at the mention of his name, and a warmth spread through me, frustratingly undeniable. "Darcy? He's insufferable. Condescending and rude." I recounted our encounter, skimming over the more intimate details of our heated exchange, the way his eyes had lingered on me, the electric tension that had crackled between us.

"And yet," Jane said, a knowing smile playing at her lips, "you can't seem to stop thinking about him, can you?"

I opened my mouth to retort, to deny the ridiculous notion, but the sound of the shop bell interrupted me. Speak of the devil. Darcy himself stepped through the door, his presence commanding the space instantly. He moved with a purposeful grace, his eyes scanning the shelves before settling on me with a smoldering intensity that sent a shiver down my spine. It lasted only a moment but the effects were lingering.

"I'm looking for a moldavite crystal," he said, his voice low and smooth, resonating through me like a dark melody. His gaze was piercing, holding mine with a mix of challenge and something deeper, something that made my pulse quicken and my resolve waver.

My breath caught in my throat, and for a moment, I was rooted to the spot, unable to tear my eyes away from him. His presence filled the shop, thickening the air between us with a tension so palpable that it was almost suffocating. I could feel

the heat rising in my cheeks, the maddening awareness of him that I couldn't seem to shake.

As I led him to the display, every step felt like a
battle against the pull that drew me toward him, a
magnetic force that made it nearly impossible to
focus on anything but the man at my side. My skin
tingled with awareness of his proximity, and I
fought the urge to reach out, to touch him, to close
the maddening distance between us. It was infuriating.

"Here it is," I said, my voice slightly breathless as I
gestured to the selection of moldavite crystals. "Is
there a specific one you're looking for?"

Darcy's eyes flicked to the display, but I could feel
his attention still fixed on me, as if he were studying
me, trying to decipher the thoughts I was so desperately trying to keep hidden. "I trust your judgment,
Miss Bennet," he replied, his tone deceptively calm.
"You seem to have a discerning eye."

There was an undercurrent to his words, a subtle
challenge that made my heart skip flutter. I reached
for one of the crystals, my fingers brushing his as I
handed it to him. The contact sent a jolt of electricity through me, and I had to suppress a gasp. His
eyes flicked up to meet mine, dark and hungry, and
for a moment, it felt as though the world had

narrowed to just the two of us, caught in a web of desire and frustration.

"This one should suit your needs," I managed to say, my voice barely above a whisper. I could feel my composure slipping, the heat between us threatening to consume me.

Darcy held the crystal, his gaze never leaving mine. "Thank you," he said, his voice a low rumble that sent another shiver down my spine. He lingered a moment longer, his eyes burning into me, before he finally turned his attention to my sisters, who had been watching the entire exchange with thinly veiled curiosity.

"Ladies," Darcy said, inclining his head in a gesture that was both courteous and commanding. "I would like to extend an invitation to the Netherfield Ball. My friend Mr. Bingley and I would be honored if you would join us."

The invitation hung in the air, and for a moment, I could only stare at him, my mind struggling to process his words through the haze of desire that clouded my thoughts.

Jane's eyes lit up with delight, a soft smile spreading across her face. "We would be delighted, Mr. Darcy. Thank you for the invitation."

Lydia, ever the enthusiast, practically bounced

with excitement. "Oh, I can't wait! A ball at Nether-field! It's going to be the event of the season!" She shot me a teasing grin, her eyes sparkling with mischief. "I suppose even you can't turn this one down, Lizzy."

I forced a smile, my heart still racing from the intensity of Darcy's gaze. "Of course not," I replied, though my thoughts were far from the excitement of the ball. My mind was consumed by the man standing before me, by the way his presence seemed to ignite a fire within me that I couldn't control, couldn't ignore.

"Then it's settled," Darcy said, his voice a velvet caress that sent another wave of heat through me. "We shall look forward to your company."

With that, he turned to leave, but not before his gaze flicked back to me one last time, lingering on my face, as if memorizing every detail. The door swung shut behind him, and I let out a shaky breath, feeling as though I had just emerged from a storm.

My sisters watched him go, their expressions a mix of curiosity and something unspoken. I knew they had felt it too, the undeniable pull between us, the storm brewing on the horizon. But they said nothing, perhaps sensing that this was something beyond their understanding, something that was meant to remain unspoken.

As the door closed behind Darcy, I felt a surge of frustration and desire, a need that burned hotter with every encounter. I was caught between the desire to fan the flames and the need to keep them at bay, between the longing to be near him and the fear of what that might mean.

This was far from over. The fire Darcy ignited within me was not something that could be easily extinguished. And as much as I tried to tell myself that it was nothing, that he was nothing more than a frustrating, insufferable man, I knew in my heart that I was lying to myself. The truth was, I wanted him. And that want was growing stronger with every passing moment, threatening to consume me entirely.

But as I turned back to my sisters, I forced those thoughts aside, burying them deep where they couldn't hurt me.

For now, I would focus on the ball, on the promise of a night filled with magic and mystery. But deep down, I knew that no matter how hard I tried, I couldn't ignore the fire that burned within me, a fire that only Darcy seemed to be able to ignite.

5

ELIZABETH

*T*he warm glow of the candles hanging from the enchanted chandeliers above us cast flickering shadows across the grand hall at Netherfield, but I barely noticed as I glided across the dance floor with George Wickham. His charming smile, his light touch—it was all so effortless, so natural, that I found myself completely at ease in his company despite my earlier reservations. The soft hum of magic surrounded us, interwoven with the music, making each step feel like part of a spell designed to captivate and enthrall.

We hadn't known each other long—only a few months, in fact. He'd arrived in town with little fanfare, but it hadn't taken him long to win over nearly everyone. Wickham had a way of making you feel like the most important person in the room, his attention so focused, his charm felt so genuine, that it was impossible not to be drawn in. He had woven himself into the fabric of the town effortlessly, as if he had always belonged, always been a part of our world.

But tonight, there was something different about him. Something more… intense. The way he looked at me, the way his hand rested just a bit too low on my back—it sent a thrill of something I couldn't quite name down my spine. It was as though he was trying to cast a spell of his own, one that was working far too well.

As we danced, I caught sight of Darcy standing across the room. His gaze was fixed on us, his expression unreadable, but there was a tension in the way he held himself, his usual stoic demeanor slipping just for a moment. His eyes, sharp and piercing, seemed to darken as they locked onto mine. A flicker of something—disapproval, jealousy, or perhaps something deeper—crossed his features before he quickly looked away.

Wickham, ever attuned to the people around him, seemed to sense the shift in the room, and his smile widened, though it didn't quite reach his eyes. "It seems Mr. Darcy is watching us rather closely," he murmured, his voice low and intimate, as if we were sharing a secret. "I wonder what he could be thinking."

His tone was light, but there was an undercurrent to his words that made me pause. Wickham had always been charming, always quick with a smile or a kind word, but there was something calculated in his demeanor tonight, as if he were playing a part in a game I didn't fully understand.

"He often watches, but rarely speaks," I replied, trying to keep my tone just as light. "Perhaps he's simply observing."

Wickham chuckled softly, his breath warm against my ear. "Or perhaps he's considering his next move. Darcy is not a man to take lightly, you know. He's… particular about whom he associates with."

There it was again, that subtle edge to his words, a hint of something more beneath the surface. Wickham was a master at making friends, at ingratiating himself with those around him, but I couldn't shake the feeling that there was more to his charm than met the eye. He had a way of making you feel special, of making you trust him implicitly, and yet… there was always something just out of reach, something he kept hidden behind that easy smile.

As the dance ended, Wickham bowed low, his

eyes never leaving mine. "Thank you for the dance, Miss Bennet. It was, as always, a pleasure."

I smiled back, but my mind was racing. Wickham had charmed his way into our lives so effortlessly, but now, I couldn't help but wonder if there was a purpose to his actions, a scheme behind his seemingly innocent flirtations. Darcy's gaze lingered on us for a moment longer before he turned away, his expression once again unreadable.

As I watched Wickham move on to charm the next person in his sights, a sense of unease settled over me. He was too smooth, too perfect in his movements, and the way he had integrated himself into the town in just a few short months felt almost... deliberate.

Whatever Wickham was up to, I couldn't shake the feeling that he was playing a long game, one where every move was calculated, every smile a carefully placed piece on the board.

As I watched Wickham move on to charm the next person in his sights, a sense of unease settled over me. He was too smooth, too perfect in his movements, and the way he had integrated himself into the town in just a few short months felt almost... deliberate. Whatever Wickham was up to, I couldn't shake the feeling that he was playing a long game, one where every move was calculated, every smile a carefully placed piece on the board. And somehow, I was caught in the middle of it.

My thoughts were still tangled in the web of Wickham's intentions when I caught sight of Darcy across the room. He was standing near the entrance, his tall, imposing figure unmistakable even from a distance. His presence was a stark contrast to Wickham's; where Wickham was all charm and warmth, Darcy was cold, distant, like a fortress guarded by high walls.

I tried to tear my eyes away, but there was something magnetic about him, something that held me in place. The crowd seemed to part for him as he moved through the room, and for a moment, I thought I saw his gaze flicker in my direction. My heart stuttered, and I quickly looked away, trying to ignore the way my pulse quickened at the mere thought of him noticing me.

But then, as if the universe were conspiring against me, Darcy moved closer, his path bringing him near where I stood. I forced myself to focus on the conversation between the witches nearby, but my body betrayed me, every nerve alight with the awareness of his proximity. The air around me seemed to thicken, the very atmosphere charged with a tension that was almost unbearable.

Just as he passed by, his arm brushed against mine—so subtle, so fleeting that it could have been unintentional, but the effect was immediate and undeniable. Heat shot through me, burning a path from the point of contact down to the pit of my stomach, where it pooled like molten lava. My breath hitched, my body responding with a trai-torous thrill that I struggled to suppress.

He didn't stop, didn't even glance in my direc-tion, but continued on as if nothing had happened, as if he hadn't just set my entire body aflame with a simple, accidental touch. The venom that rose to my lips was almost instinctual, a defense mechanism against the overwhelming desire that pulsed through me. How dare he affect me so? How dare he walk away as if I were nothing?

My hand curled into a fist at my side, the fire in my veins mingling with the bitter taste of disdain. I hated the way he made me feel—so exposed, so vulnerable to his presence. And yet, the intensity of my reaction only seemed to deepen the pull he had on me, drawing me into a storm I wasn't sure I could weather.

Wickham, noticing my brief distraction, leaned

in closer, his voice soft enough that it felt like a secret between us. "You know, Miss Bennet, I can't help but notice your reaction to our dear Mr. Darcy earlier."

I raised an eyebrow, trying to play off the sudden flutter in my chest at the mention of Darcy's name. "And what reaction might that be, Mr. Wickham?"

He chuckled, the sound rich and warm, carrying with it the faintest hint of enchantment. "The one where you looked like you'd rather be anywhere else in the world than in his presence."

I forced a smile, though my heart was still racing from the encounter. "Perhaps that's because I would. Mr. Darcy has a way of making one feel most unwelcome."

Wickham's gaze sharpened, his smile turning sly. "Or perhaps, Miss Bennet, there's more to it than that. Sometimes the things we resist most are the things that have the strongest hold on us."

I stiffened, a cold prickle of unease running down my spine. His words felt too close to the truth, too perceptive for comfort. I wanted to deny it, to laugh off the suggestion, but the fire still smoldering within me made it impossible. Instead, I met Wickham's gaze with as much calm as I could muster. "You're quite the observer, Mr. Wickham, but I assure you, there's nothing to concern yourself with where Mr. Darcy is involved."

Wickham's smile remained, but his eyes glinted with something sharper, more calculating. "May I have this dance, Miss Bennet?"

I sighed, a smile tugging at the corners of my lips despite myself. I took his hand as he led me to the dance floor.

Mr. Wickham spun me gracefully in time with the music. As we twirled, I felt a brief pulse of magic from Wickham, subtle and controlled, keeping perfect time with our movements. "But you're not alone, you know. There are many who feel the same way about Darcy, myself included."

That piqued my curiosity. "Oh? And why is that?"

Wickham's expression sobered slightly as he led me toward the edge of the dance floor, away from prying eyes and ears. The room's enchanted walls muted the sounds around us, creating a bubble of privacy that allowed his words to reach me alone. "It's not something I talk about often," he admitted, "but I feel that you, of all people, deserve to know the truth."

I tilted my head, intrigued. "The truth?"

He nodded, his gaze drifting briefly toward the far end of the room where Darcy stood, conversing with Bingley. The candles near them flickered as if reacting to an unseen energy. "Darcy and I... we have a history, one that doesn't reflect well on him, I'm afraid."

We found a quiet corner, and Wickham leaned against the wall, his demeanor suddenly serious. I could sense that this was not just idle gossip, but something deeply personal, something that had left its mark on him in more ways than one. The air around us was thick with magic in the room that seemed to still in response to his tale. I folded my arms and waited, giving him the space to speak.

"I'm sure you've heard of Darcy's family, the Darcys of Pemberley," Wickham began, his voice low. "A powerful line of sorcerers, wealthy, influential... and utterly ruthless when it comes to protecting their legacy."

I nodded, recalling the stories my mother had told us about the Darcy family, gossip in the town. They were one of the oldest magical families in England, known for their strict adherence to tradition and their vast wealth. Pemberley itself was said to be a place of immense power, its lands imbued with ancient magic.

"Well," Wickham continued, "my father was their steward. If you remember, I grew up alongside

Darcy, practically as brothers. We were close—at least, I thought we were. But as we grew older, it became clear that Darcy viewed our friendship differently. To him, I was always the lesser, the outsider, despite our shared upbringing."

I frowned, my heart softening at the hint of bitterness in Wickham's voice. I could already sense where this story was going, but I waited for him to finish. His aura, usually warm and inviting, flickered with traces of unresolved hurt and anger, emotions that he kept carefully controlled.

"When my father passed away," Wickham said, his gaze distant, "he left behind a small inheritance for me. Nothing compared to what the Darcys possessed, but it was enough to set me up in the world. However, when I came of age, Darcy—out of sheer spite—denied me that inheritance. He claimed that my father's will was invalid, that the money rightfully belonged to the Darcy estate."

I felt a surge of anger on Wickham's behalf, my own aura flaring in response. "But that's… that's terrible! How could he do that?"

Wickham smiled sadly, a flicker of pain in his eyes. His aura dimmed slightly, the warmth fading. "Because he could. Because he's Fitzwilliam Darcy, and he's used to getting what he wants, no matter the cost to others."

I shook my head, the warmth I had briefly felt toward Darcy quickly cooling. "And you haven't been able to challenge him?"

"I tried," Wickham admitted, "but Darcy's connections run deep. The legal battles were... expensive, and in the end, I was left with nothing. No inheritance, no position in the magical world. I've had to rebuild my life from scratch."

I could barely contain my indignation. "That's monstrous! How could anyone be so cruel?"

Wickham sighed, placing a hand on my arm in a gesture of comfort. His touch sent a ripple of calming magic through me, soothing the anger he had stoked. "It's just the way he is, Elizabeth. Darcy is proud, arrogant, and utterly convinced of his own superiority. He sees people like you and me as beneath him, unworthy of his time or respect."

I clenched my fists, my mind racing with everything Wickham had told me. It confirmed all my worst suspicions about Darcy, solidifying the impression I had formed of him as cold, heartless, and insufferably arrogant. And yet... I couldn't shake the feeling that there was more to the story, something deeper lurking beneath the surface, something that Darcy kept hidden behind his carefully constructed facade.

But even as doubt crept in, I pushed it aside. Wickham's story was compelling, and the pain in his voice had been real. If Darcy could treat someone he had once called a friend so callously, then he was every bit the villain Wickham made him out to be.

"I'm so sorry, George," I said, genuinely moved by his story. "You didn't deserve that."

He smiled, though it didn't quite reach his eyes. "Thank you, Elizabeth. It means a great deal to me that you understand."

We rejoined the gathering, and I found myself glancing at Darcy with a newfound wariness. If he was capable of such cruelty, I needed to protect myself—and my family—from whatever schemes he might have in store. The enchantments in the room seemed to dim slightly as I watched him, as if even the magic sensed the tension between us.

As I watched him from across the room, my gaze met his, and for a fleeting moment, the world seemed to narrow down to just the two of us. The look in his eyes was intense, and I could almost feel the weight of his stare, as if he were trying to see through my defenses, to understand something even I couldn't grasp. There was a brief flicker of something—an emotion I couldn't quite name—before he turned away, breaking the connection.

But that moment lingered with me. I couldn't deny the power Darcy seemed to have over a room, nor could I dismiss the unsettling way my heart raced whenever our paths crossed. It was infuriating, confusing, and utterly impossible to ignore. Yet, as much as I wanted to despise him, a small, unwelcome part of me couldn't help but wonder if there was more to Fitzwilliam Darcy than met the eye.

As the evening wore on, I sought out Jane, who was still deep in conversation with Bingley. When I finally managed to pull her aside, she noticed the tension in my expression immediately.

"Lizzie, what's wrong?" she asked, her brow furrowing with concern. Her usually bright and calm aura, flickered with worry.

"I just spoke with George Wickham," I replied, keeping my voice low. "He told me some things about Darcy... things that make me think we need to be careful around him."

Jane's eyes widened. "What did he say?"

I relayed Wickham's story as succinctly as I could, watching Jane's face for her reaction. She listened intently, but when I finished, she seemed hesitant to jump to conclusions. Her aura remained steady, its warmth tinged with concern but not the anger I had felt.

"Lizzie," she began gently, "I understand why you're upset, but are you sure you have the full story? Sometimes… well, sometimes things aren't as simple as they seem."

I shook my head, frustrated by her reluctance to believe Wickham's account. "Jane, he was clearly hurt by what Darcy did to him. How could he lie about something like that?"

"I'm not saying he's lying," Jane replied, her tone measured, "but people's perceptions can be influenced by their emotions. Maybe there's more to what happened between them."

"Or maybe Darcy is exactly what he appears to be —a cold, arrogant man who only cares about himself," I shot back, crossing my arms. "I'm just saying we should be careful. I don't want you getting hurt, Jane."

Jane sighed, her expression thoughtful. "I appreciate your concern, Lizzie. I really do. But I think it's important to give people the benefit of the doubt. At least until we know more."

I wanted to argue further, but I knew Jane was too kind-hearted to judge anyone harshly. It was one of her most endearing qualities, even if it sometimes frustrated me to no end. Her aura pulsed gently, a reminder of her innate goodness.

Before I could respond, the atmosphere in the room changed suddenly. The lighthearted chatter faded, replaced by a subtle tension that crackled in the air like static electricity. The magic in the room seemed to pulse with awareness, sensing the presence of something—or someone—significant. I turned, and there, standing at the entrance, was George Wickham—his charming smile still in place, but his eyes locked on someone else.

The moment Darcy and Wickham locked eyes, the atmosphere shifted from mere tension to something much darker, almost oppressive. The warm light of the room dimmed as if the very air was absorbing the energy between them. The once bright chandeliers flickered, casting eerie shadows that seemed to stretch and distort, creeping across the walls like tendrils of dark magic.

A low, almost inaudible hum filled the space, the sound of power crackling just beneath the surface, waiting to erupt. The guests, who had moments before been animated and lively, fell silent, their voices stolen by the sudden change in the room. They instinctively backed away, creating a wide berth around the two men, as if the space between them was sacred—or cursed.

Wickham's eyes glinted with something more sinister than his usual charm, a predatory gleam that matched the dangerous curve of his smile. He exuded an aura of confidence, but there was something more there—a darkness that lurked just beneath his smooth exterior. His magic pulsed subtly, sending faint sparks skittering across the floor like restless spirits.

Darcy, on the other hand, stood as still as a statue, his features carved from stone. His aura was no less powerful, but it was colder, more controlled, like the deep, unforgiving chill of winter. The air around him seemed to vibrate with barely contained energy, and though he made no move, it was clear he was ready for whatever Wickham might unleash.

The tension between them was more than just personal—it was magical, ancient, as if their very bloodlines were warring in that silent standoff. The air grew thicker, harder to breathe, as though the room itself was closing in, suffocating under the weight of their mutual loathing.

Without a word, Darcy's gaze hardened, and for a split second, the temperature in the room plummeted. Frost began to form on the edges of the windows, creeping inward like icy fingers. Wickham's smile flickered, a brief crack in his façade, but it was enough to show the strain beneath his mask.

Then, as suddenly as it began, Darcy turned on his heel and strode out of the room. The door closed behind him with a definitive thud that echoed in the silence. The room remained frozen in that moment of aftermath, the tension hanging in the air like a sword poised to drop.

Wickham's charm wavered, his eyes flicking toward the door where Darcy had disappeared, before he plastered his smile back on, the veneer of casual indifference barely hiding the fury beneath. The guests slowly began to murmur, their conversations subdued, as if they were afraid to break the fragile peace that had been restored.

But the memory of that moment lingered, the taste of magic still bitter on my tongue. Something had passed between those two men, something far darker and more dangerous than mere rivalry. And I knew, deep in my bones, that whatever it was, it was far from over.

As the night wore on, I couldn't shake the feeling that I was missing something vital, some piece of the puzzle that would make everything make sense. The magic in the room felt restless, as if it too was searching for answers. But until I had all the answers, one thing was clear: Fitzwilliam Darcy was not to be trusted.

And I would be damned if I let him hurt the people I cared about.

Yet, despite the anger Wickham had stoked within me, a small, nagging voice at the back of my mind urged caution. Wickham's story, while compelling, had been one-sided. As much as I wanted to believe him, I couldn't ignore the possibility that his own emotions had colored his perspective. After all, people often remembered events in ways that favored themselves. Perhaps there was more to the story than what Wickham had shared.

6

DARCY

The ballroom at Netherfield Hall was a sea of light and color, the polished marble floors gleaming beneath the warm glow of countless candles. The air was thick with the mingling scents of perfume and magic, the latter weaving invisibly through the crowd, sparking against the polished surfaces and casting a soft shimmer over the revelers. For most, it was a night of celebration, of dancing and laughter. But for me, it was a night of conflict, a night where restraint warred with a desire that had become impossible to ignore.

As I stood at the edge of the room, my gaze kept drifting—unbidden, unwelcome—to Elizabeth Bennet. She was across the room, her laughter ringing out in a way that cut through the noise, reaching me like a siren's call. She was captivating, a force of nature that defied the neat, orderly life I had built for myself. Her magic was untamed, her spirit wild and free, and it drew me to her like nothing else ever had.

She was dressed in a gown that clung to her curves in a way that made my mouth go dry, the fabric whispering over her skin as she moved with a grace that was almost feline. The flickering candle-light played tricks with the shadows, highlighting the delicate lines of her collarbone, the soft swell of her breasts, the curve of her hips. It was a torture to watch her, to feel my blood heat as she moved, completely unaware of the effect she was having on me.

Elizabeth was unlike any woman I had ever encountered—fiercely intelligent, quick-witted, and utterly infuriating. She challenged me at every turn, pushed me in ways that no one else dared. And it was driving me mad.

As I watched her, my desire for control slipped, the iron grip I held over my impulses loosening with every glance. I wanted her. Wanted to bend her to my will, to tame that wild spirit and make her submit to me. But even as the thought crossed my mind, I knew that Elizabeth was no ordinary woman. She would resist, fight me every step of the way, and that thought only made me want her more.

I could feel myself harden just watching her, the tension in my body coiling tight, like a spring ready to snap. Every look she gave me, every challenging tilt of her chin, every flash of defiance in her eyes was like a spark to dry tinder, igniting something primal within me that I could no longer suppress.

Unable to stay on the sidelines any longer, I crossed the room, moving with purpose, my gaze locked on her. The crowd seemed to part before me, and in moments, I was standing in front of her, the rest of the world falling away. Her eyes met mine, and the challenge in them was unmistakable.

"Miss Bennet," I murmured, my voice low, rough with the desire that I could no longer hide. "I see you're enjoying the ball."

She arched an eyebrow, her lips curving into a smirk that sent a fresh wave of heat through me. "Indeed, Mr. Darcy. And you? Are you here to survey the festivities from afar, or have you decided to grace us with your presence?"

I stepped closer, invading her space, and was rewarded with the slightest hitch in her breath. "I find I cannot stay away," I confessed, my voice a dark promise. "You draw me in, Elizabeth. I want to know what goes on behind those clever eyes of yours, what thoughts fill your mind when you look at me."

She met my gaze with a defiance that only served to stoke the fire within me. "And why should I share my thoughts with you, Mr. Darcy? Perhaps I enjoy keeping you guessing."

I leaned in, my lips brushing the shell of her ear, my breath warm against her skin. "I don't think you know what you're playing with, Elizabeth. You challenge me, provoke me, and it takes every ounce of control I have not to take you right here, right now."

She shivered, the flush on her cheeks deepening as my words sank in, but she didn't back down. Instead, she lifted her chin, her eyes locking onto mine with a fire that matched my own. "And what would you do if I let you?" she whispered, her voice a mix of bravado and curiosity.

I let my hand slide down her arm, barely brushing the fabric of her gown, but enough to make her pulse quicken. "I would make you mine," I growled softly. "I would strip you of that defiance, teach you what it means to submit, to surrender to me completely. I would have you on your knees, begging for me, and you would love every second of it."

Her breath caught, and for a moment, I saw the

uncertainty in her eyes, the war between her desire and her need to remain in control. "You think so?" she challenged, though her voice wavered ever so slightly.

"I know so," I replied, my hand moving to the small of her back, pulling her just a fraction closer. "You want it too, Elizabeth. I see it in the way you look at me, the way you react when I'm near. You want to feel my hands on you, my mouth on you, to hear my voice as I tell you all the things I'm going to do to you."

She swallowed hard, her bravado faltering as the reality of my words settled over her. But even now, she refused to back down completely. "You're awfully confident, Mr. Darcy. But what makes you think I would ever give you that power over me?"

I let my fingers trace the curve of her spine, leaning in until my lips were just a breath away from hers. "Because, Elizabeth, I can see the way you burn for me. You may fight it, but deep down, you know you want it. You want me to take control, to push you to your limits and then take you even further. You want to surrender, to let go of that control you cling to so desperately. And when you finally do... it will be exquisite."

She was trembling now, her breath coming in

short, shallow gasps, and I could see the war raging within her—the desire to give in, to let me take her, battling against the part of her that wanted to stay in control. But as I watched her, I knew it was only a matter of time. The pull between us was too strong, the fire too hot to resist for long.

But then, just as I thought she might yield, she pulled back, her expression hardening as she regained control over herself. "You may think you know me, Mr. Darcy," she said, her voice laced with venom, "but you don't. I'm not some conquest for you to claim, and I won't be tamed by anyone."

With that, she turned on her heel and walked away, leaving me standing there, my body aching with the need to go after her, to finish what we had started. But even as she moved away, I knew that this was far from over. The fire that burned between us was too strong, too consuming to be extinguished by a few harsh words.

No, this was only the beginning. And when the time came, when she finally gave in to what we both wanted, it would be everything I had promised and more. Because I would make sure of it.

"Darcy, you look positively morose," Bingley's voice interrupted my thoughts, pulling me back to the present. He appeared at my side, a glass of wine in hand and a broad smile on his face. The air around him hummed with a subtle, warm magic— Bingley's aura was always soothing, a stark contrast to the storm that raged within me. "This is supposed to be a celebration, remember? Why aren't you enjoying yourself?"

I forced a smile, though it felt strained. "I'm perfectly fine, Bingley. Just... observing."

Bingley followed my gaze and chuckled. "Observing, eh? Or perhaps brooding?"

I gave him a pointed look, but Bingley was undeterred. "If I didn't know better, I'd say you have your eye on someone." His grin widened as his gaze landed on Elizabeth. "Ah, I see."

"You see nothing," I muttered, irritated by how easily Bingley had read me.

"Oh, but I do," he said, his tone teasing. "And I think you should stop overthinking everything for once and simply enjoy yourself."

I turned to him, my expression serious. "Bingley, there are things you don't understand. Elizabeth Bennet is..."

"Lovely," he interrupted, raising an eyebrow. "Charming, intelligent, and completely unattached. What exactly is the problem, Darcy?"

I sighed, running a hand through my hair in frustration. "The problem is that she's unsuitable. Her family, her lack of refinement, the way she wields her magic without understanding the full extent of its power—she's not... she's not like us."

Bingley's smile faded slightly, and he regarded me with a mixture of disappointment and pity. "Not like us? Darcy, I think you underestimate her. Elizabeth Bennet is far more than she appears. And I dare say, so are you."

Before I could respond, the music swelled, and Bingley clapped me on the shoulder. "Come now, it's a ball! Ask her to dance, Darcy. You might be surprised."

He was gone before I could protest, leaving me standing there, grappling with the turmoil of my thoughts. The idea of asking Elizabeth to dance felt both impossible and inevitable, like a spell already cast, waiting to be fulfilled.

How could I let this happen? How could I allow myself to be drawn to someone so unsuitable, so beneath the standards I had set for myself? And yet, the more I tried to push her from my mind, the more firmly she lodged herself there, her presence a constant, unyielding force.

I knew what was expected of me—a match with someone of equal standing, someone who understood the intricacies of our world, who could navigate the delicate balance of power that defined our lives. Elizabeth Bennet was not that person. She was too wild, too unpredictable, too... everything I shouldn't want.

And yet, as I watched her from across the room, her laughter ringing out like a melody that only I could hear, I knew that my carefully constructed world was beginning to crumble.

And so, before I could talk myself out of it, I crossed the room to where Elizabeth stood. She noticed my approach, her smile faltering as she met my gaze with those sharp, discerning eyes. Her aura flickered with curiosity, mingled with the faintest hint of suspicion.

"Miss Bennet," I greeted her with a slight bow, my voice carefully controlled. "May I have the honor of this dance?"

She hesitated, and for a moment, I feared she might refuse. But then she gave a small nod, her expression unreadable. "Very well, Mr. Darcy."

I offered her my hand, and as our fingers touched, I felt a jolt of something—magic, perhaps, or simply the electricity that seemed to crackle between us whenever we were near. Her magic responded to mine, a sudden flare of energy that sent a thrill through me. I led her to the dance floor, conscious of the eyes that followed us, and tried to ignore the tightening in my chest.

The music began, and we moved together in time with the rhythm, our steps precise and measured. But it didn't take long for the tension to build, our magical energies clashing in a way that was almost tangible. Elizabeth's magic was wild, untamed—like a force of nature, unpredictable and powerful. My own magic was the opposite, carefully controlled, honed through years of discipline. The two energies swirled around us, neither one yielding, creating a palpable friction.

Elizabeth's brow furrowed slightly as she seemed to sense the conflict, her gaze flickering up to meet mine. There was a challenge in her eyes, a silent dare that only fueled the turmoil within me.

"Is something the matter, Mr. Darcy?" she asked, her voice laced with subtle defiance.

"Not at all, Miss Bennet," I replied, my tone betraying none of the frustration I felt. "Why do you ask?"

She tilted her head, her lips curling into a faint, almost teasing smile. "You seem rather... preoccupied."

I nearly scoffed at the irony of her words, but I

held my composure. "Merely focused on the dance, Miss Bennet."

Her smile widened slightly, and she looked away, her gaze drifting across the room. "I see. Well, I do appreciate your focus. Though I must say, I'm surprised you asked me to dance."

I raised an eyebrow. "Why is that?"

"Because," she said, meeting my eyes once more, "you seem to go out of your way to avoid me."

There was a sharpness to her words that caught me off guard, and for a moment, I struggled to find a response. How could I explain that avoiding her was my only defense against the inexplicable pull I felt toward her? That every moment in her presence threatened to unravel the carefully constructed barriers I had built around myself?

Instead, I chose a safer response. "Perhaps I've simply been... cautious."

"Cautious?" she repeated, a note of incredulity in her voice. "Of what, Mr. Darcy? Surely you don't think I'm dangerous."

Her teasing tone belied the intensity of her gaze, and I felt the tension between us heighten. Dangerous? No, she wasn't dangerous in the way she meant. But she was dangerous to me—to everything I thought I knew, everything I thought I wanted. Her presence made my control waver, my carefully guarded emotions threaten to spill over.

"I think," I began slowly, "that you are more complex than I initially realized."

Her expression softened for a moment, surprise flickering across her features, but it was quickly replaced by her usual guarded demeanor. "And I think, Mr. Darcy, that you are more difficult to understand than you let on."

The music began to draw to a close, and I realized that we had danced through the entire piece without either of us truly enjoying it. There was no ease between us, no connection—only a battle of wills and a clash of forces that left me feeling more unsettled than ever.

But before the music could completely die down, Elizabeth leaned closer, her breath warm against my ear. "Tell me, Mr. Darcy," she whispered, her voice low and charged with something I couldn't quite place, "do you truly believe that control is the pinnacle of magic? That restraint is more powerful than freedom?"

Her question caught me off guard, the intimacy of the moment sending a shiver down my spine. The way she said it, with such quiet intensity, made my pulse quicken. There was something seductive in her words, a challenge that went beyond mere debate.

I looked down into her eyes, the deep brown pools drawing me in despite my every instinct to resist. "Yes," I replied, my voice equally soft but firm. "Control is what separates us from the chaos. It's what makes magic truly formidable."

Elizabeth smiled, a slow, knowing smile that made my heart pound. "Perhaps, Mr. Darcy, but sometimes, it's the chaos that brings about the most profound change. It's the unrestrained power, the passion, that truly shapes the world."

Her words hung in the air between us, the tension so thick it was almost suffocating. I was acutely aware of her proximity, of the way her magic seemed to pulse in time with her heartbeat, challenging my every belief, every deeply held conviction. I couldn't decide if I wanted to pull her closer or put as much distance between us as possible.

But then, in a moment of sheer madness, I found myself leaning in, my lips brushing against the shell of her ear as I spoke. "You make it difficult, Elizabeth. You make it impossible to focus on anything but you." My voice dropped lower, the raw desire in my tone unmistakable. "Do you know how hard you make me? How I can barely stand in your presence without wanting to bend you over my knee and spank that defiance out of you?"

Her breath hitched, and I could feel the tremor that ran through her, but she didn't pull away. Instead, she turned her head slightly, her lips so close to mine that I could almost taste her. "And what else would you do, Mr. Darcy?" she asked, her voice a breathy whisper that sent fire racing through my veins.

My hand tightened around hers, the pressure just enough to let her know that I wasn't playing games. "I would strip you bare," I growled softly, "taste every inch of your body until you scream my name. I would bury my tongue in your cunt, make you beg for mercy while I take my time, savoring every moment. And then, when you can't take it anymore, I would fuck you until you're nothing but a trembling, pleading mess beneath me."

Her eyes darkened with desire, her lips parting slightly as if she were imagining every word I had just said. But even now, she wouldn't give in completely. "You talk a good game, Mr. Darcy," she murmured, her voice laced with a challenge. "But I wonder... are you all talk?"

I leaned in closer, my lips brushing against hers for the briefest of moments before I pulled back, leaving her wanting more. "You'll find, Miss Bennet, that I'm a man of action as well as words. And when the time comes, you'll know exactly what it means to submit to me."

The music ended, the final notes lingering in the air as I released her hand, stepping back just enough to let the tension between us simmer. She stared at me, her eyes still clouded with desire, and I knew that this was far from over. We were both playing a dangerous game, one that could easily spiral out of control.

But for now, I was content to leave her wanting, to let the anticipation build until the moment we both knew was inevitable finally arrived.

7

JANE

The garden at Netherfield had always been a place of peace for me, a sanctuary where I could lose myself among the flowers and the gentle hum of nature. But today, it felt different. The air was charged with something I couldn't quite name, a sense of anticipation that made my heart flutter in my chest.

Charles walked beside me, his presence warm and comforting, but there was an undercurrent of tension that I couldn't ignore. We strolled through the garden paths, the sun casting long shadows as it dipped toward the horizon. The flowers seemed to glow in the golden light, their colors more vibrant than ever. I could feel the magic in the air, a gentle pulse that resonated with the happiness swelling in my chest.

But there was something more, something that lingered between us, unspoken but undeniable. I knew I needed to tell him the truth—not about being a witch, which he already knew and accepted—but about the circumstances of my life. The truth of my family's financial struggles, of how I worked in my parents' shop, Bennet's Charms & Curiosities, to help make ends meet.

"Charles," I began, my voice soft but steady, "there's something I need to tell you."

He turned to me, his eyes warm and attentive, and I could see the affection in his gaze. "What is it, Jane?"

I took a deep breath, gathering my courage. "My family… we're not as well off as some might think. My parents run a small shop, and I help them with it. It's not just a pastime for me—it's necessary. We're not wealthy, and I've always known that if I want something in life, I have to work for it."

He didn't react with surprise or pity, only understanding. "Jane, that only makes me admire you more. The fact that you're willing to work hard, to support your family… it speaks to your character, your strength. It doesn't change how I feel about you. In fact, it only makes me care for you more."

His words sent a thrill through me, and I turned to face him, my heart pounding. "You're not… disappointed?"

He shook his head, his eyes locked on mine. "Not at all. I'm honored that you trust me enough to share this with me. You're extraordinary, Jane, in every way."

Before I could respond, Charles took my hand and brought it to his lips, pressing a soft kiss to my fingers. The tenderness of the gesture, combined with the warmth in his eyes, made my breath catch. It was as if the world around us had faded away, leaving only the two of us, standing in the twilight, connected by something deeper than words.

"I've never felt this way before," Charles confessed, his voice thick with emotion. "Being with you, it's like… it's like I've found something I didn't even know I was looking for."

My heart swelled at his words, and I stepped closer, the space between us disappearing as I reached up to touch his face. "I feel the same way, Charles. You've given me more than I could have ever hoped for."

He smiled, his eyes shining with a mixture of affection and desire. "Jane, I don't think I can hold back any longer."

And then, before I could respond, his lips were on mine. The kiss was gentle at first, tentative, as if he were afraid of overwhelming me. But as I wrapped my arms around his neck and pressed myself closer to him, it deepened, becoming something more intense, more urgent.

The world around us seemed to pulse with energy, the magic in the air responding to our connection. My skin tingled where his hands touched me, and I felt a warmth spread through me, starting at my core and radiating outward. It was unlike anything I had ever experienced, a heady mix of emotion and sensation that left me breathless.

Charles's hands moved to my waist, pulling me even closer, and I could feel the heat of his body against mine. The intensity of the moment was overwhelming, and I felt a rush of emotions—desire, love, a deep, undeniable need for him.

As the kiss deepened further, I felt his hands begin to explore, tracing the contours of my body with a reverence that made my heart race. My dress slipped slightly under his touch, and I gasped, a mixture of surprise and pleasure shooting through me. I had never felt anything like this before, and the sensations were almost too much to bear.

"Jane," Charles whispered against my lips, his voice rough with desire, "You're so beautiful... I've never wanted anyone the way I want you."

His words sent a shiver down my spine, and I felt a heat rise in me, a need that I had never known before. I could hardly believe what was happening, that this man—so kind, so gentle—could stir such intense feelings within me.

We continued to kiss, our movements growing more urgent, more passionate. I could feel his hands on my back, slowly unlacing my dress, and a thrill of excitement shot through me. It was as if all my fears, all my insecurities, had melted away, leaving only the pure, unadulterated need to be close to him.

"Charles," I breathed, my voice trembling with a mixture of anticipation and nervousness, "I've never... done this before."

He paused, pulling back slightly to look at me, his expression softening with tenderness. "You're incredible, Jane. And I want you to know that you can trust me. I'll take care of you, I promise."

The sincerity in his voice, the love in his eyes, made me feel safe, secure in a way I had never felt before. I nodded, unable to speak, and he smiled, brushing a strand of hair from my face before kissing me again.

The kiss quickly grew more heated, more intense, and I felt my body responding in ways I hadn't anticipated. His hands continued to explore, finding my breasts and teasing them in a way that sent waves of pleasure through me. I moaned softly, unable to hold back the sounds of my own desire, and he responded by deepening the kiss, his lips moving to my neck, trailing soft kisses along my skin.

We moved together, our bodies pressing closer, the tension between us building with every touch, every kiss. I felt his hand slide down my back, lifting the hem of my dress, and I shivered as his fingers brushed against the sensitive skin of my thigh.

"Do you trust me, Jane?" he whispered, his voice thick with desire.

"Yes," I breathed, my mind spinning with the intensity of the moment.

He smiled, his eyes dark with passion, and then he was lifting my skirts, lowering me to the ground with a gentleness that belied the urgency of our actions. I felt the cool earth beneath me, contrasting with the heat of his body as he settled between my legs.

He began to kiss me again, his mouth moving lower, tracing a path down my body until he reached the place where I needed him most. A place only I had ever touched before. I gasped as I felt his tongue on me, the sensation unlike anything I could have ever imagined. It was sweet, intense, and overwhelming, and I could hardly believe that this was happening, that I was experiencing this with him.

"You taste like strawberries and honey," Charles murmured against me, his voice full of wonder. "So sweet, so delicious."

His words sent another shiver through me, and I felt a tension begin to coil in my belly, building with each stroke of his tongue. He found my nub, the one spot that made me see stars, and I moaned, my hands fisting in the fabric of my dress as I writhed beneath him.

The pleasure was almost too much, and I felt myself climbing higher and higher, the tension building to a peak that I could hardly comprehend. Just when I thought I couldn't take any more, he slid a finger inside me, and I almost cried out in surprise and pleasure.

"More," I gasped, unable to stop myself. "Please, Charles, more."

He obliged, slipping another finger inside me, his

mouth never leaving that sensitive spot. The combination of sensations was too much, and I felt the tension finally snap, sending me spiraling into an orgasm that left me trembling with its intensity.

I cried out his name as the pleasure washed over me, wave after wave, and he continued to work me through it, his movements slow and deliberate, drawing out every last bit of sensation.

But he wasn't done. As I lay there, spent and breathless, he moved up to kiss me again, his lips soft and gentle against mine, before trailing his kisses down my neck, to my collarbone, and lower. He positioned himself between my legs, his breath warm against my skin as he kissed his way down, until he was tasting me again, driving me wild with the intensity of his desire.

He added another finger, stretching me in the most delicious way, and I felt the pleasure build again, faster this time, more urgent. His tongue moved in tandem with his fingers, teasing and tasting, driving me to the edge once more.

"Charles, I... I can't..." I gasped, my body trembling with the intensity of the sensations coursing through me.

"Yes, you can, Jane," he whispered against my

skin, his voice filled with reverence and lust. "I want to feel you come apart for me again."

And I did. The second orgasm hit me even harder than the first, tearing through me with a force that left me gasping for breath, my hands gripping his hair as I rode the waves of pleasure.

When it was over, I lay there, spent and trembling, my body still quivering from the aftershocks of pleasure. Charles slowly moved back up to me, his eyes filled with an intensity that made my heart race all over again. He kissed me softly, his lips lingering on mine as if savoring the moment.

"Jane," he murmured, his voice thick with emotion and desire, "you're incredible."

I smiled up at him, feeling a warmth spread through my chest that had nothing to do with the physical pleasure we had just shared. It was deeper, more profound—a connection that went beyond mere attraction or lust. It was love, pure and simple, and it filled me with a sense of completeness that I had never known before.

Charles brushed a strand of hair from my face, his touch tender and reverent. "I've never felt this way before," he confessed, his voice barely above a whisper. "I've never wanted someone as much as I want you, Jane. You're everything I've ever dreamed of, and more."

Tears welled up in my eyes at his words, and I reached up to cup his face in my hands. "And you're everything to me, Charles. I've never felt so... cherished, so loved."

He smiled, his expression softening with affection. "You are cherished, Jane. You're everything to me."

We kissed again, this time slower, savoring the connection between us. The world around us seemed to disappear, leaving only the two of us, entwined in each other's arms. The passion that had ignited between us hadn't diminished; if anything, it had grown stronger, more intense. But now, it was tempered with something deeper, something that made the moment all the more meaningful.

As we lay there, tangled together, the night settled around us, the stars beginning to peek through the twilight sky. The garden, once a place of peace, had become something more—a place of love, of discovery, of new beginnings.

And as I rested my head against Charles's chest, listening to the steady beat of his heart, I knew that whatever challenges lay ahead, we would face them together. Because this was more than just a passionate encounter. It was the beginning of something extraordinary, something that would change both our lives forever.

With a contented sigh, I closed my eyes, letting the warmth of his embrace and the love in his eyes wrap around me like a comforting blanket. I was home, in every sense of the word.

8

WICKHAM

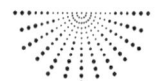

he fire crackled softly in the dimly lit room, the only sound in an otherwise silent night. The Netherfield Ball had been a success —better than I could have anticipated. Elizabeth Bennet had already begun to fall into my carefully laid trap, and soon, her foolish sister Lydia would follow. But before I turned my full attention to Lydia, there was another matter to attend to—one that required a darker, more dangerous touch.

I stood from the chair, the warmth of the fire no longer comforting, but stifling. Tonight, I intended to push the boundaries, to delve into forbidden spells that most sorcerers wouldn't dare touch. But I was not like most sorcerers. I had spent years perfecting my craft, honing my skills in secret, away from the prying eyes of those who would judge me for it.

As I crossed the room, my hand grazed the edge of the small wooden table where I had prepared the tools for tonight's ritual. A black candle, its wick already singed from previous uses, stood at the center, surrounded by a circle of salt and dried herbs —ingredients carefully chosen for their potency in dark magic. Next to the candle, a small vial of blood-red potion glimmered ominously, the liquid inside swirling with an energy that seemed almost alive.

But the true centerpiece of the ritual was the ancient, leather-bound tome that lay open on the table. Its pages were filled with spells long forgotten by the magical community—spells that could bend the will of others, twist reality to the caster's desires, and even bring forth forces from the beyond. I had spent years searching for this book, and now that it was in my possession, I intended to use it to its full potential.

My eyes skimmed over the incantation on the page, the words written in a language older than any known to most sorcerers. They were harsh, guttural, and filled with power—power that had been outlawed centuries ago for its danger and unpre-dictability. But that was exactly what I needed.

I began the ritual, lighting the black candle and placing my hands over the tome. The words flowed from my lips, ancient and powerful, filling the room with a dark energy that crackled in the air. The candle's flame flickered, almost as if it were alive, reacting to the magic that was being summoned. I could feel the power building, coiling within me like a serpent ready to strike.

As the spell reached its climax, I uncorked the vial and poured a single drop of the potion onto the open page. The liquid hissed as it touched the paper, and the room was suddenly filled with a thick, acrid smoke. I didn't flinch, my focus entirely on the task at hand. The smoke began to take shape, forming a dark, swirling cloud that hovered above the book, pulsating with malevolent energy.

"Come forth," I commanded, my voice low and commanding. "Show me your power."

The cloud responded, its shape solidifying into a shadowy figure, indistinct but undeniably present. Its presence filled the room with a chilling cold, a stark contrast to the warmth of the fire. The figure had no face, no features—only darkness, but its power was palpable, pressing down on me like a physical weight.

"I seek control," I continued, my voice unwavering. "The ability to bend others to my will, to make them see what I want them to see, believe what I want them to believe."

The figure remained silent, but I felt its acknowledgment, a subtle shift in the air that told me I had its attention. This was not a simple conjuring—it was a pact, a bargain struck with forces that most sorcerers would never dare to approach. But I was willing to take the risk. I had nothing left to lose, and everything to gain.

"Bind them to me," I intoned, "and I will give you what you desire."

The figure seemed to grow larger, more defined, as it absorbed the words of the incantation. The room grew colder still, and I could feel the magic wrapping itself around me, tightening like a noose. It was dangerous, yes, but that was the point. I needed power—real power—to take down Darcy and claim what was rightfully mine.

As the ritual reached its peak, the figure suddenly surged forward, its essence merging with mine. I gasped as the cold, dark energy flooded my body, filling me with a strength and power unlike anything I had ever felt before. It was intoxicating, overwhelming, and utterly exhilarating.

But with that power came a price—a price I was willing to pay.

The figure's presence began to fade, retreating back into the ether, but the power it had granted me remained, coursing through my veins like liquid fire. I could feel it settling into my very soul, a permanent mark of the bargain I had struck.

Yet as I stood there, savoring the sensation, a sharp, searing pain shot through my chest, nearly doubling me over. The intensity of it stole my breath, and for a moment, I thought I might collapse. The pain radiated from my heart, spreading through my body like a wildfire, leaving a trail of burning agony in its wake.

Gritting my teeth, I forced myself to stand upright, clutching the edge of the table for support. The pain was a side effect—a warning of the dangers I had invited into my life. Dark magic always came with a cost. The power I had gained was intoxicating, yes, but it was also a poison, slowly working its way through my veins, tainting everything it touched.

But I couldn't afford to stop now. The stakes were too high, and I had already come too far. I would bear the consequences of my actions, whatever they might be, as long as they brought me closer to my goal.

As the pain subsided to a dull ache, I extinguished the candle and began to clean up the remnants of the ritual, my mind turning to Lydia Bennet. She was the perfect target for this newfound power—naive, eager to please, and desperate for adventure. A few well-placed spells, a touch of dark magic, and she would be mine to control. And once she was, I would have the leverage I needed to strike at Darcy where it hurt most.

But Lydia was just the beginning. There would be others—people who had underestimated me, who had dismissed me as nothing more than a charming rogue. They would soon learn the truth, and by then, it would be too late.

As I prepared to leave, I couldn't help but smile. The game was only just beginning, and I intended to play it to the fullest. Fitzwilliam Darcy had no idea what was coming. And when the time came, he would fall—just like everyone else who had ever underestimated me.

THE NEXT DAY, I MADE MY WAY THROUGH THE VILLAGE of Meryton, my mind still buzzing with the remnants of last night's ritual. I had never felt more powerful, more in control. The villagers greeted me with their usual smiles and pleasantries, completely unaware of the dark magic that pulsed beneath my charming exterior. It was almost too easy, slipping into the role of the affable gentleman while hiding the monster within.

I stopped at the market square, where a young vendor was selling fruits and vegetables. He was a lanky boy, no more than sixteen, with an eager expression that made him look even younger. He caught sight of me and grinned, holding up a basket of fresh apples.

"Good morning, sir! Would you like some apples? They're the best in Meryton!"

I smiled, but it was a cold, calculated smile. The boy had no idea who he was dealing with, and that made it all the more enjoyable. "They look delicious," I said, stepping closer. "But I'm afraid I don't have any coins on me today."

The boy's smile faltered, but he quickly recovered, nodding enthusiastically. "That's all right, sir! You can pay me next time. Or... perhaps you could trade me something?"

I raised an eyebrow, feigning interest. "A trade, you say? And what would you like in return?"

The boy hesitated, his eyes darting to the side as if he were afraid of being overheard. "Well, sir… I've heard stories. Stories about you."

"Is that so?" I replied, my tone deceptively light. "And what kind of stories might those be?"

He leaned in closer, lowering his voice. "They say you're a sorcerer. A powerful one. I was wondering if… if maybe you could teach me something. Just a small spell, nothing dangerous. I want to impress a girl, you see."

I chuckled softly, though there was no warmth in the sound. "Ah, young love. How charming."

The boy beamed, completely unaware of the trap he had just walked into. I pretended to consider his request, tapping my chin thoughtfully. "Very well," I said at last. "I'll teach you a spell. But you must promise to keep it a secret. Magic is not something to be trifled with, and there are those who would not approve of such… experiments."

The boy's eyes lit up, and he nodded eagerly. "I promise, sir! I won't tell a soul!"

I leaned in closer, my voice dropping to a whisper. "Repeat after me…"

I recited a simple incantation, one that would create a small, harmless burst of light. The boy's face lit up with excitement as he repeated the words, and when a faint spark of light appeared in his hand, he let out a delighted laugh.

But the spark was only the beginning. I had woven a darker spell into the incantation, one that would slowly drain the boy's energy over time, leaving him weaker and more susceptible to my influence. It was a subtle spell, one that he would never notice until it was too late.

The boy thanked me repeatedly in an annoying fashion, still pleading as he handed me the basket of apples. I accepted them with a nod, watching as he hurried off to show his newfound power to the girl he hoped to impress.

I knew it wouldn't be long before the spell began to take its toll on him. He would grow weaker, more tired, until he was little more than a puppet, ready to be controlled by the master who had given him the gift of magic.

As I made my way back to the inn where I was staying, I couldn't help but feel a sense of satisfaction. This was what real power felt like—bending others to my will, using their own desires against them. The boy was just the first. There would be others, each one helping to pave the way for my ultimate goal.

And Lydia Bennet would be next.

I found her in the garden at Longbourn, twirling a small charm in her hands. She looked up as I approached, her face lighting up with a smile that was both innocent and eager.

"Mr. Wickham!" she exclaimed, hurrying over to me. "I was just thinking about you!"

"And what a lovely thought that must have been," I replied smoothly, taking her hand and pressing a kiss to it. "You are the very picture of beauty this morning, Miss Lydia."

She giggled, clearly pleased by the compliment. "You're too kind, Mr. Wickham. But I have to tell you—I've been practicing the spell you taught me."

"Oh?" I said, feigning surprise. "And how has that been going?"

She blushed, looking down at the charm in her hands. "Well, I think I'm getting better. But it's still not quite right. I was wondering if… if maybe you could help me?"

I smiled, like taking candy from a babe. "Of course, my dear. I would be more than happy to assist you."

We spent the next hour practicing the spell, though I made sure to weave in subtle suggestions and manipulations with each incantation. Lydia was so eager to learn, so desperate to please, that she

JAX WILDER

didn't even notice the way my influence was seeping into her mind, wrapping around her like a vise.

By the time we finished, she was completely under my spell—literally and figuratively. She would do anything I asked, without question, without hesitation.

And that was exactly what I needed.

As I left the garden, I couldn't help but feel a sense of triumph. Lydia Bennet was mine to control, and with her in my grasp, the Bennet family would be easy prey.

The game was only just beginning, and I intended to play it to the fullest.

92

9

LYDIA

The excitement of the Netherfield Ball had hardly worn off when I found myself seeking out George Wickham at every opportunity. There was something about him—his easy smile, his charming manners, the way he made me feel as though I was the only person in the room—that drew me in like a moth to a flame. I knew my sisters, especially Lizzie, would scold me for being too forward, but I couldn't help it. Wickham was different. He made me feel alive, important, and seen.

It wasn't long before our encounters became more frequent. He would seek me out during walks, and we would stroll through the gardens, talking about everything and nothing. His presence was intoxicating, and I found myself hanging on his every word, eager to impress him.

One afternoon, as we walked through a secluded part of the woods near Longbourn Hollow, Wickham suddenly stopped and turned to me, his eyes dark and intense. The playful smile that usually graced his lips was gone, replaced by a serious expression that made my heart skip a beat.

"Lydia," he began, his voice low and velvety, "there's something I've been meaning to show you. Something special."

I looked at him, curiosity piqued. "What is it, Mr. Wickham?"

He smiled then, a slow, almost predatory grin that sent a shiver down my spine. "It's a little bit of magic," he said, reaching into his coat and pulling out a small, ornate vial filled with a shimmering liquid. The liquid seemed to pulse with a dark, hypnotic energy, and I found myself unable to look away.

"What is it?" I asked, my voice barely above a whisper.

"This," Wickham explained, holding the vial up to the light, "is a potion of attraction. It's a rare and powerful elixir that can amplify the feelings of those who drink it. Just a drop, and the person you desire will find themselves drawn to you, unable to resist your charms."

I stared at the vial, my heart racing with a mix of excitement and trepidation. The idea of having such power over someone, of making them fall hopelessly in love with me, was both thrilling and terrifying. But Wickham's voice was so smooth, so convincing, that I found myself nodding along, entranced by the possibilities.

"Would you like to try it?" he asked, his eyes boring into mine with an intensity that made my pulse quicken.

I hesitated, the rational part of my mind screaming at me to say no, to walk away. But Wickham's gaze was so compelling, so full of promise, that I couldn't bring myself to refuse. I nodded, my voice trembling as I spoke.

"Yes, I would."

Wickham's smile widened, and he uncorked the vial, pouring a single drop of the shimmering liquid into his hand. He extended it toward me, and I stared at it, my heart pounding in my chest.

"Go on," he urged softly. "Just a drop. It won't harm you."

With a deep breath, I reached out and dipped my finger into the liquid. It was warm, almost unnervingly so, and as I brought it to my lips, I felt a strange tingle run down my spine. The taste was sweet, like honey, but with an undercurrent of something darker, something I couldn't quite place.

As the potion took effect, I felt a sudden rush of warmth flood my body, and my senses seemed to sharpen. The colors around me became more vivid, the sounds of the forest more pronounced. And when I looked at Wickham, it was as though a veil had been lifted—I saw him not just as a charming rogue, but as the most handsome, most desirable man I had ever encountered.

He stepped closer, his eyes locking onto mine with a smoldering intensity that made my breath catch. "How do you feel, Lydia?"

"I... I feel..." I struggled to find the words, overwhelmed by the surge of emotions coursing through me. "I feel amazing."

Wickham chuckled softly, his hand brushing a strand of hair from my face. "That's the power of the potion, my dear. It heightens everything—your senses, your desires. And it makes you even more irresistible."

I blushed under his gaze, a heady mix of embarrassment and exhilaration flooding my veins. The way he looked at me, the way he spoke to me—it was like nothing I had ever experienced before. I felt powerful, confident, and completely in his thrall.

But then, in a momentary lapse, I saw something in Wickham's eyes—something cold, calculating, and almost cruel. It was gone in an instant, replaced by his usual charm, but the glimpse was enough to send a flicker of unease through me.

As if sensing my hesitation, Wickham's expression softened, and he took my hand in his, his touch gentle and reassuring. "Lydia, you have nothing to fear. This magic is just a tool, a way to help you achieve your heart's desires. And I'm here to guide you."

I wanted to believe him, to trust in the warmth of his smile and the comfort of his words. But the memory of that cold, dark look lingered in the back of my mind, a shadow that refused to be banished.

Wickham leaned in closer, his voice a husky whisper that sent shivers down my spine. "Do you want more?"

"Yes," I breathed, the word escaping my lips before I could stop it.

Wickham's smile widened, and he reached into his coat, producing another vial of the shimmering liquid. He held it out to me, and I took it eagerly, my hands trembling with anticipation.

"Drink this," he instructed, his voice a soft command. "It will bind our hearts together, make our connection unbreakable."

I hesitated for only a moment before uncorking the vial and downing its contents. The liquid was warm and sweet, like the first, but this time, the effects were immediate and overwhelming. A surge of heat flooded my body, and I felt as though I was on fire, my senses heightened to an almost unbearable degree.

Wickham stepped closer, his hand caressing my cheek as he leaned in to whisper in my ear. "You're mine now, Lydia. And I'm yours. Forever."

His words sent a shiver down my spine, and I closed my eyes, surrendering completely to the moment, to him. I didn't care about anything else—not the warnings Elizabeth had given me, not the nagging doubts in the back of my mind. All that mattered was the way Wickham made me feel—alive, desired, and completely under his spell.

But then, as if some dark force had been unleashed within him, Wickham's grip on my hand tightened painfully, and his eyes flashed with something dangerous, something malevolent.

"Lydia," he said, his voice a low growl, "you will do exactly as I say, won't you?"

The sudden shift in his tone, the hard edge to his words, sent a wave of fear through me. I nodded quickly, too frightened to do anything else.

"Good," Wickham murmured, his voice softening once more as he released my hand. "Because I have plans for you, my dear. Plans that will change everything."

As he spoke, I could feel the effects of the potion working their way through me, clouding my thoughts, dulling my instincts. The unease I had felt moments before was fading, replaced by a sense of helplessness, of submission.

And in that moment, I realized the full extent of Wickham's power over me. He wasn't just charming or persuasive—he was dangerous, capable of manipulating me in ways I hadn't even begun to comprehend.

But it was too late. I was already ensnared in his web, bound to him by the dark magic he wielded so effortlessly. And as we continued our walk through the woods, the world around us fading into the background, I knew that there was no escape from the path I had chosen.

Wickham had me, body and soul. And there was nothing I could do to stop him.

10

ELIZABETH

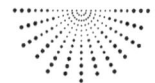

The sun hung low in the sky, casting a warm, golden hue over the estate as I strolled through the gardens of Longbourn. The quietude of the late afternoon was a welcome respite from the whirlwind of thoughts that had plagued me since the Netherfield Ball. My mind was a tumultuous storm of confusion, unease, and something else—something I was not yet ready to name.

I had come out to clear my head, to make sense of the swirling emotions that Darcy's behavior had stirred within me. His anger at the ball, his cryptic warnings about Wickham, his intense gaze that seemed to pierce through my very soul—none of it made sense. And yet, I couldn't shake the feeling that there was something deeper beneath the surface, something he wasn't telling me.

As I turned a corner in the garden, following the path lined with blooming roses, I stopped short. There, standing in the shade of a large oak tree, was Mr. Darcy. He was alone, his posture rigid, his expression unreadable as he looked out over the fields that stretched beyond the garden. He hadn't noticed me yet, and for a moment, I considered turning back, avoiding the confrontation that I knew was inevitable. But the questions burning in my mind would not allow me to retreat.

Gathering my resolve, I stepped forward, the sound of my footsteps on the gravel path catching his attention. He turned to face me, his eyes narrowing slightly as they met mine.

"Miss Bennet," he greeted me, his voice as calm and composed as ever. But there was a tension in his gaze, a flicker of something unspoken that made my heart pound.

"Mr. Darcy," I replied, my voice steady despite the turmoil churning inside me. "I did not expect to see you here."

"I might say the same of you," he responded, his tone cool and measured. "It seems we are both seeking solace in the gardens today."

I hesitated for a moment, unsure of how to broach the subject that had been weighing on my mind since the ball. But the need for answers was too great, and I knew I could not leave without confronting him.

"Mr. Darcy," I began, my voice firm, "there is something I must ask you."

He inclined his head slightly, signaling for me to continue.

"Why were you so angry with Mr. Wickham at the Netherfield Ball?" I asked, the words coming out more sharply than I had intended. "What is it about him that provokes such a strong reaction in you?"

For a moment, Darcy said nothing, his expression hardening as he considered my question. When he finally spoke, his voice was low and controlled, but there was an unmistakable edge to it.

"Wickham is not the man he appears to be," he said, his eyes darkening with barely concealed emotion. "He is a liar and a manipulator, and I have seen firsthand the damage he can cause."

His words sent a shiver down my spine, but I refused to let him see how much they affected me. "That may be so," I replied, "but your actions that night were more than just concern for my well-being. You were furious, Mr. Darcy. And I want to know why."

Darcy's jaw tightened, and I could see the struggle in his eyes as he fought to maintain his composure. "You don't know the full extent of what he has done," he said, his voice strained. "If you did, you would understand why I cannot stand by and let him continue his deceit."

"Then tell me," I challenged, stepping closer. "Tell me what it is that you know."

For a moment, I thought he might finally open up, might finally reveal the truth that I so desperately sought. But then his expression hardened once more, and he shook his head.

"It is not that simple," he said, his tone laced with frustration.

"Of course, it's not," I muttered, my own frustration bubbling to the surface. "You always speak in riddles, Mr. Darcy. Always so certain of your own superiority, of your ability to judge others. But perhaps the real reason you hate Wickham is that he mirrors something in yourself that you despise."

His eyes flashed with anger, and I saw the muscles in his neck tense as he struggled to keep his temper in check. "You know nothing about me, Miss Bennet," he said, his voice low and dangerous. "You think you can read me, understand me, but you are woefully mistaken."

"Then enlighten me," I shot back, my own anger flaring. "Tell me what it is you're so afraid of."

For a moment, neither of us spoke, the tension between us crackling like lightning in the air. Then, without another word, Darcy turned on his heel and stormed off, leaving me standing there, breathless and shaking.

As I watched him disappear down the path, I felt a mix of anger, confusion, and something else— something that made my heart ache in a way I couldn't quite understand. This was far from over, and I knew that the answers I sought were still out of reach. But I also knew that I couldn't let this go. I would find out the truth, no matter what it took.

THE NEXT MORNING, I FOUND A LETTER WAITING FOR me on my dressing table. The seal was unmistakable —Darcy's family crest, the intricate design pressed into the wax with a precision that spoke of his rigid control. My heart pounded as I picked it up, my fingers trembling slightly as I broke the seal and unfolded the parchment.

The letter was long, and as I began to read, I

could feel the weight of Darcy's words pressing down on me.

Elizabeth,

You asked me for the truth, and though I know it may not change your opinion of me, I cannot let you continue to believe the lies Wickham has spun.

Wickham and I have known each other since childhood. My father was fond of him, and for a time, I considered him a friend. But as we grew older, it became clear that Wickham's charm was merely a facade, hiding a man with a dangerous appetite for power and dark magic. My father left him a legacy in his will, believing that Wickham would use it to better himself. Instead, Wickham squandered the money on gambling and debauchery, and when he came to me asking for more, I refused.

It was then that his true nature revealed itself. Wickham sought out magical artifacts—relics of our family, meant to be kept safe and secure. He used these artifacts to dabble in dark magic, to manipulate and control those around him. The last time he attempted such a feat, he nearly succeeded in taking over a small town, influencing its inhabitants to do his bidding. I had to step in to stop him, and in doing so, I showed him a mercy that, in hindsight, I should not have extended.

You see, Elizabeth, he tried to possess my sister. His intent was to use her as a vessel for his twisted ambitions, to corrupt her mind and soul. It took all of my power to free her from his grasp, and I swore then that I would never allow him to harm another innocent. That is why I am here in Longbourn Hollow. I came because I heard whispers of his return, and I cannot allow him to wreak havoc once more.

I know that you see me as cold, as proud and unfeeling. But you must understand that my actions are driven by the need to protect those I care about. I could not stand by and let Wickham deceive you as he has deceived so many others.

I apologize for the harshness of my words, for the way I have treated you. It was never my intention to wound you, but I find it increasingly difficult to control myself in your presence. You drive me wild, Elizabeth. Your spirit, your defiance—it stirs something in me that I can barely contain. The thought of you, of your body, your voice, haunts my every waking moment.

You make it impossible to focus on anything but the desire that burns within me, a desire that I fear will consume us both if left unchecked.

I do not expect your forgiveness, nor do I ask for it. I only ask that you believe me when I say that my actions, however misguided, are born from a place of deep care and concern.

F. Darcy

I READ THE LETTER TWICE, MY MIND REELING WITH the revelations it contained. The truth about Wickham, Darcy's role in protecting his sister, and the raw, unfiltered confession of his desire for me— it was all too much to process at once.

But one thing was clear: Darcy was not the man I had thought him to be. He was more—more complicated, more passionate, more dangerous than I could have ever imagined.

And as much as I wanted to deny it, to push him away, I knew that I was already too far gone. The fire that burned between us was real, and it was only a matter of time before it consumed us both.

With a trembling hand, I folded the letter and placed it back on the table, my heart racing with a mixture of fear and anticipation.

11

ELIZABETH

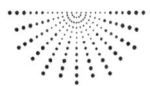

The day had passed in a haze, my thoughts consumed by Darcy's letter. Each word lingered in my mind, stirring emotions I had tried to bury. The weight of his confession, the revelation of his desires—it was too much to process, too much to ignore. By evening, my restlessness had become unbearable.

Dressed in a simple robe, I left my room, the letter clutched tightly in my hand. The house was quiet, the only sound the soft hum of magic that permeated Longbourn. I needed space to think, to confront the storm inside me. My feet carried me through the dimly lit corridors until I found myself walking through the garden.

A faint light spilled out from around the side of the building. I wasn't alone. My heart raced as I turned the corner, my breath catching when I saw him. Darcy stood by the window, bathed in the pale glow of the moonlight. His usual composure was gone, replaced by a restless energy that mirrored my own.

"Miss Bennet," he said quietly, turning to face me. His voice was low, laced with an emotion I couldn't quite place.

"Mr. Darcy," I replied, stepping closer. The air between us was thick with tension, the weight of everything unsaid pressing down on us.

"Hello, I..." he ran a hand through his tousled hair, his eyes searching mine. "Is there something I can do for you?"

"I didn't expect to see you here," I said. It was my family's property after all.

"Right. I was uh, going for a walk," he said motioning for me to follow deeper into the garden.

I hesitated, the letter crumpling slightly in my hand. "I read your letter," I began, my voice faltering. "And I realize now that I was wrong about you."

Darcy's expression tightened, a flicker of something—fear, perhaps—crossing his face. "There is no need to apologize, Miss Bennet. I understand why you felt as you did."

"No," I insisted, taking a step closer. "You don't understand. I accused you of things, judged you without trying to comprehend your reasons."

His gaze softened, and he took a hesitant step toward me, the tension crackling like electricity. "I have made mistakes," he admitted, his voice strained. "But I never intended to harm you or your family."

"I know that now," I whispered, my heart pounding as we stood only a breath apart. The air between us was charged, the pull of his presence irresistible.

For a moment, I thought he might reach out to touch me. Instead, he clenched his fists, struggling to maintain control. "Elizabeth," he began, his voice thick with emotion, "there are feelings I can no longer suppress."

My heart skipped a beat, the world spinning slightly as I realized what he was trying to say. "Mr. Darcy…"

"Please," he interrupted, his voice rough with desperation. "Let me speak."

I nodded, my breath hitching as I waited for him to continue.

"I have fought against these feelings for so long," he confessed, his words tumbling out. "But I cannot rid myself of them. I am drawn to you, Elizabeth, in ways that defy reason."

Everything felt heavier, charged with the intensity of his confession. My own resolve crumbled, the walls I had built around my heart shattering.

"Say that you forgive me," he murmured, stepping closer until our bodies almost touched. "Say that you understand."

I opened my mouth to respond, but the words caught in my throat. Instead, I found myself leaning in, drawn to him by a force I couldn't resist. The tension between us was unbearable, the need to touch him overwhelming.

And then, our lips met.

The kiss was gentle at first, tentative, as if we were testing the waters. But it quickly deepened, the intensity of our emotions spilling over into something raw and unrestrained. His hands found my waist, pulling me closer as I melted into him, my own hands tangling in his hair.

He pressed me against a tree, his body flush against mine, the heat of him seeping into me. His lips trailed down to my neck, sending shivers of pleasure through me.

"Elizabeth," he murmured against my skin, his voice rough with desire. "You don't know what you do to me. You don't know the things I want to do to you."

My throat went suddenly dry. "I'm not afraid. I want you too. Show me," I whispered, my voice trembling with anticipation.

His eyes darkened, the control he usually wielded slipping as his desire took hold. "Undress for me," he commanded, his voice low and authoritative. "Now."

A thrill shot through me at his words, my body responding to his command. But I hesitated, my breath catching as I met his gaze, challenging him.

His eyes narrowed, a dangerous edge creeping into his voice. "If you disobey, you'll be punished," he warned, his tone sending a shiver down my spine.

I swallowed hard, the heat between my legs growing unbearable as I slowly began to untie the robe. But before I could let it fall, I hesitated again, a small act of defiance.

Darcy's gaze darkened further, and before I could react, he had me over his knee, his hand coming down sharply on my ass. The sting was swift, but the pleasure that followed was overwhelming. I gasped, my body arching against him as he delivered another, then another, each one sending a jolt of pleasure through me.

"You're a brat, Elizabeth," he growled. "But you're mine."

He lifted me back to my feet, his eyes blazing as he slowly began to undress me, piece by piece. Each removal of clothing was a reward, a slow, tantalizing stripping of my defenses. His hands roamed over my exposed skin, his touch electrifying.

When I was finally bare before him, he stepped back, his gaze raking over me with a hunger that made me tremble.

"You've been a good girl," he murmured, his voice sending a fresh wave of desire through me. "Now, let me reward you."

He dropped to his knees before me, his hands parting my thighs as he leaned in, his mouth finding my most sensitive spot. The first touch of his tongue made me cry out, the sensation so intense it was almost too much. He licked and sucked at my clit, his hands holding me steady as he brought me to the edge of ecstasy.

I was panting, gasping his name as the pleasure built inside me, each stroke of his tongue driving me closer to the edge. And then, with a cry, I came, the orgasm ripping through me with a force that left me trembling.

But he didn't stop. He continued to tease me, his mouth relentless as he slipped a finger inside me, then another, stretching me as he drove me to another orgasm. My body was on fire, the pleasure so intense it bordered on pain.

"I have to make sure you're ready," he whispered against my skin, his fingers moving inside me with a skill that made me moan. "Ready for me."

I could only nod, my mind lost to the sensations as he continued to work me, his mouth and hands pushing me to the brink again and again. When my body exploded a third time, I was sobbing with plea-sure, my body shaking with the force of it.

He rose then, his eyes dark with lust as he posi-tioned himself between my legs. "I'm going to enter you now, Elizabeth," his voice low and commanding. "And you're going to take me like the good girl you are."

I could only whimper and nod my head enthusi-astically. I wanted him, my body aching with need as he slowly slid inside me, the sensation of being filled so completely sending me spiraling into another orgasm. His size, his thickness, stretched me, the pleasure mingling with a sweet pain that made me gasp.

"No man has ever touched me like this," I confessed, my voice trembling.

He paused, his eyes searching mine as he pressed a kiss to my lips. "Then let me be the first," he whispered, "and the only."

He began to move, slow at first, but soon picking up speed as he drove into me, each thrust hitting a spot inside me that made me see stars. The pleasure was indescribable, the feeling of him inside me, the way he filled me so completely, overwhelming.

"Come for me," he growled, his hand slipping between us to rub my clit. "Come for me, Elizabeth."

I couldn't hold back, my body responding to his command as another orgasm tore through me. I cried out, the sound muffled only by the magic that surrounded us, a silence bubble that kept our world contained.

He didn't stop, his movements growing more frantic as he chased his own release. Pleasure crashed over me like a tidal wave as I felt him spill inside me, his heat flooding my core.

When it was over, we were both breathless, our bodies tangled together in a way that felt both intimate and possessive. He pressed a kiss to my forehead, his voice a low rumble as he whispered, "You're mine, Elizabeth. No one else will ever touch you. You're mine, and I'm yours."

The words sent a shiver through me, the truth of them settling deep in my bones. I was his, completely and utterly, and nothing would ever change that.

Not now, not ever.

12

LYDIA

*T*he twilight sky bled into deep purples and reds as I made my way to the secluded clearing Wickham had shown me. My heart raced with excitement and a touch of fear. Ever since that first drop of the attraction potion Wickham had shared with me, I felt a hunger for more—more power, more magic, more of him. It was a thrill unlike anything I had ever experienced, and I wanted to dive deeper, to see how far this new world of dark magic could take me.

But there was a part of me that was nervous, a part that remembered the warnings from Lizzie, who had always been the cautious one. She had told me tales of witches who had dabbled too deeply in dark magic, only to lose themselves completely. I had brushed off her concerns at the time, eager to embrace this new side of life that Wickham had opened up for me, but now, as I approached the clearing, those warnings seemed to echo in my mind.

Wickham had become my guide, my mentor in these forbidden arts. He had shown me things that made the simple charms and spells I learned at home seem like child's play. The magic he wielded was dangerous, intoxicating, and I was completely under its spell. But was I ready for what tonight would bring? Was I truly prepared to sacrifice a part of myself for this power?

I reached the clearing and found Wickham already there, standing beside a small altar he had constructed from stones and wood. The air around him seemed to pulse with energy, dark and alluring. He looked up as I approached, a smile playing on his lips.

"Lydia," he greeted me, his voice smooth and velvety. "Right on time. Are you ready for tonight's lesson?"

I nodded eagerly, but the nerves buzzing in my stomach made my voice come out softer than I intended. "Yes, Mr. Wickham. What are we doing tonight?"

His smile widened, and he beckoned me closer. "Tonight, we're going to take your magic to the next level. You've already shown a natural talent for the arts I've introduced you to, but there's so much more you can achieve."

I stepped closer, my eyes fixed on the altar. It was adorned with various objects: black candles, a bowl of shimmering liquid, and an old, tattered book that looked like it had seen centuries of use. The pages of the book were yellowed and worn, the ink faded in some places, but the power emanating from it was undeniable.

"What is that?" I asked, pointing to the book.

"This," Wickham said, running his fingers lightly over the cover, "is a grimoire—an ancient book of spells and rituals passed down through generations of powerful sorcerers. It contains knowledge that most witches and warlocks would kill for. And tonight, Lydia, you will be the one to wield that power."

A shiver of excitement ran through me. The idea of using such ancient and forbidden magic was thrilling, but a part of me hesitated. I had always been warned about the dangers of dark magic, about how it could consume those who used it recklessly.

But with Wickham by my side, those fears seemed distant, insignificant.

"What do I have to do?" I asked, my voice barely above a whisper.

Wickham's eyes gleamed with approval. "First, you must understand that the magic in this book is not like the simple spells you've been taught. It requires a sacrifice, a part of yourself, to fuel the power it holds. Are you willing to make that sacrifice, Lydia?"

I swallowed hard, the gravity of his words sinking in. This was it—the moment where I would truly step into the world of dark magic, leaving behind the safety of the familiar. But the desire for more—more power, more knowledge, more of Wickham—was stronger than my fear.

"Yes," I said firmly. "I'm ready."

"Good," he said, his smile dark and dangerous. "Then let us begin."

He handed me the book, and I felt a jolt of energy the moment my fingers touched the worn leather cover. It was as if the book itself was alive, its power surging through me, filling me with a heady mix of fear and exhilaration.

"Open it," Wickham instructed, and I did, carefully turning the brittle pages until I found the spell he had mentioned earlier—a spell of binding, meant to tether two souls together in an unbreakable bond.

"This spell," Wickham explained, "will link our magic, our very beings, in a way that cannot be undone. It will make us stronger, more powerful, but it comes at a cost. Are you still willing?"

I hesitated, my hand hovering over the page. The words Lizzie had spoken to me before echoed in my mind—her warnings about the dangers of dark magic, about how it could corrupt and destroy. Was I making a mistake? Was I about to lose myself to something far beyond my control?

But then I looked up at Wickham, at the way his eyes gleamed with power and confidence, and the doubt melted away. He believed in me. He had chosen me to share this magic with, to stand by his side. How could I turn back now?

I nodded, pushing the doubts aside. The thought of being bound to Wickham, of sharing his power, was too enticing to resist.

He guided me through the ritual, his voice low and hypnotic as he chanted the ancient words. I followed his lead, my voice trembling at first but growing stronger with each syllable. The air around us crackled with energy, and I could feel the magic building, swirling around us like a storm.

As the spell reached its climax, Wickham took my hand and made a small cut on my palm with a silver dagger, the pain sharp but fleeting. He did the same to his own hand, then pressed our palms together, our blood mingling as the final words of the spell left our lips.

The moment the spell was complete, a shockwave of power surged through me, so intense that I gasped, my knees nearly buckling. Wickham's grip on my hand tightened, grounding me as the magic settled, intertwining our souls, our magic, in a way that felt both exhilarating and terrifying.

I looked up at him, breathless and wide-eyed, and he smiled down at me, his expression filled with a mix of pride and something darker, more possessive.

"You've done well, Lydia," he murmured, his voice thick with satisfaction. "We are bound now, you and I. Our fates are sealed together, and there is nothing—no one—who can break that bond."

I nodded, still trying to catch my breath, the reality of what I had just done sinking in. I was bound to Wickham, to his dark magic, and there was no turning back.

But instead of fear, all I felt was a deep, consuming need for more. More magic, more power, more of him.

"Teach me more," I whispered, my voice trembling with a mix of anticipation and desperation. "Show me what else I can do."

Wickham's smile widened, and he leaned down, his lips brushing against my ear as he whispered, "In time, my dear Lydia. In time. But for now, let us savor this moment. You've taken your first step into a world most can only dream of."

As the night deepened and the last remnants of daylight faded from the sky, I knew that I had crossed a line, one that could never be uncrossed. But with Wickham by my side, guiding me, I didn't care. I was ready to embrace whatever dark path lay ahead, no matter the consequences.

For the first time in my life, I felt truly powerful. And I wasn't about to let that feeling go.

13

ELIZABETH

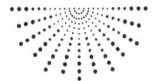

The first light of dawn filtered through the windows, casting a soft glow over the quiet kitchen. I sat alone at the table, my hands cradling a cup of tea that had long since cooled. The silence of the house was a stark contrast to the tumultuous emotions swirling within me. My thoughts drifted back to last night, to the feel of Darcy's body pressed against mine, the way he kissed me, worshipped every inch of me with a fervor that made my heart race even now. I could still feel the heat of his skin, the way he filled me so completely, the possessive way he claimed me.

And then his words echoed in my mind, the memory sharp and vivid. When I had whispered, "What if I'm with child?" his response had been low, resolute, and filled with an intensity that sent a shiver down my spine. "I hope you are. You are mine, Elizabeth."

I stirred sugar into my tea, the rhythmic motion a soothing contrast to the memories that consumed me. I was lost in the recollection, my heart still beating in time with the passion that had bound us together. The world outside had yet to stir, but inside, I was still wrapped in the heat of his embrace, the lingering taste of him on my lips, and the undeniable truth that I was irrevocably his.

The soft tap at the window startled me from my thoughts. I looked up to see a large raven perched on the sill, its dark eyes fixed intently on me. My heart sank; I knew immediately that this was no ordinary bird. In our world, ravens were often used as messengers for urgent and secretive matters, and their arrival was rarely a good sign.

With a sense of dread, I opened the window, allowing the raven to hop inside. It carried a scroll in its beak, the parchment sealed with a symbol I recognized immediately—Lydia's. My hands trembled slightly as I took the scroll and unrolled it, the message within written in a hurried, almost frantic hand:

Gone to be with George. Don't worry about me. We'll be together soon.

Lydia

My breath caught in my throat as I read the words over and over, trying to make sense of them. Lydia had run off with Wickham? How could this be? She had been in her room the night before—surely someone would have noticed if she had left.

The raven let out a low caw, as if urging me to move, to act. I jumped to my feet, the scroll slipping from my hands as I ran to Lydia's room, my heart pounding in my chest. I threw open the door, praying that I was wrong, that she would be there, safe and sound.

But the room was empty.

The bed was neatly made, the wardrobe doors slightly ajar as if they had been opened in haste. A chill ran down my spine as I realized that this was no mere disappearance—Wickham had used magic to take Lydia away, right from under our noses. How could we not have sensed it? How could we have been so blind?

Mrs. Bennet's cries of despair echoed through the house, her wails of anguish filling the air as she read the note the raven had delivered. "Oh, my poor Lydia! What will become of her? What will become of us?" she cried, wringing her hands as she paced the room. "The scandal! The shame! Our family will be ruined, ruined forever!"

Mr. Bennet, usually so calm and detached, looked pale and shaken as he tried to comfort his wife, but his own fear and uncertainty were plain on his face. "We must act quickly," he said, his voice trembling. "We must find them and bring Lydia back before it's too late."

Too late.

The words echoed in my mind, a chilling reminder of what was at stake. If Lydia and Wickham were not found, the consequences would be far worse than mere scandal. Lydia's very magic was at risk, and with it, the safety of our entire family. Wickham could hold her hostage, siphon her powers, or use her as leverage to demand anything he wanted from us.

And the worst part of it all was that I knew— deep down—I was partly to blame.

I should have seen through Wickham's lies earlier. I should have warned Lydia, should have protected her from the charm and deceit that had so easily ensnared her. But I hadn't, and now she was gone—taken by a man who would stop at nothing to get what he wanted.

Guilt gnawed at me as I stood in the middle of the chaos, my mind racing to find a solution. My parents were too distraught to think clearly, and Jane was too inexperienced to help. There was only one person who might be able to fix this, who had the power and the determination to find Lydia and bring her back safely.

Fitzwilliam Darcy.

The thought of turning to Darcy, after everything that had happened between us, filled me with a mix of dread and desperation. But I had no other choice. Lydia's life, her future, was at stake, and I couldn't let my pride stand in the way of saving her.

I left the house quickly, ignoring my mother's frantic questions and my father's worried gaze. The journey to Netherfield felt both too long and too short, the minutes ticking by as my mind raced with fear and hope.

When I arrived at Netherfield, I was greeted by a surprised servant who, after a brief hesitation, led me to Darcy's study. The door was closed, and I could hear the murmur of voices from within. My heart pounded in my chest as I waited, trying to steady my breath and gather my thoughts.

Finally, the door opened, and Darcy stepped out, his expression changing from surprise to fierce determination as he saw me standing there.

"Elizabeth," he said, his voice low but intense. There was no need for formalities now, no need for pretense. "What's happened?"

I swallowed hard, trying to keep the panic from my voice. "It's Lydia... she's run off with Wickham."

His eyes darkened, and a muscle in his jaw twitched as he processed the information. Without a word, he stepped aside, motioning for me to enter the study. Once inside, he closed the door behind us, sealing off the rest of the world.

"I should have dealt with him sooner," Darcy growled, his voice laced with anger. "That man deserves no mercy. I will do whatever it takes to bring Lydia back. You and your family will not suffer because of my past mistakes."

I opened my mouth to thank him, to explain more, but he cut me off, his tone brooking no argument. "You are mine, Elizabeth. And that means your family is mine to protect. I won't let anything happen to Lydia. I'll tear the world apart if I have to, but I will bring her back safely."

The ferocity in his voice left me breathless, a

shiver running down my spine. This was not the controlled, composed Darcy I had known before. This was a man ready to go to war, to do whatever it took to ensure the safety of those he claimed as his own.

"I… I didn't mean to put you in this position," I stammered, my emotions in turmoil. "But I didn't know who else to turn to."

He stepped closer, his gaze locking onto mine with an intensity that made my heart pound. "You did the right thing, Elizabeth. Wickham is a predator, and I will not allow him to harm your sister—or anyone else ever again. He will pay for what he's done."

Darcy's presence was overwhelming, the air between us charged with a mix of anger, protectiveness, and something else—something that made my skin tingle and my breath catch.

"There's no need for apologies," he continued, his voice softening slightly as he reached out to take my hand. "You are mine to protect, and that includes Lydia. I should have taken care of Wickham long ago, but I will make sure he never harms anyone again."

His hand was warm around mine, his grip firm and reassuring. For the first time since Lydia's disappearance, I felt a glimmer of hope, a sense that perhaps everything might be alright after all.

"Thank you," I whispered, my voice thick with emotion. "I don't know what we would do without you."

He lifted my hand to his lips, brushing a gentle kiss across my knuckles. "You'll never have to find out," he promised, his voice a low, soothing rumble. "I will find them, Elizabeth. And when I do, Wickham will face the consequences of his actions."

As Darcy released my hand and turned to begin his preparations, I felt a strange sense of calm settle over me. Darcy was in control now, and I knew that he would stop at nothing to bring Lydia back safely. And as I watched him take charge, issuing orders and summoning his allies, I realized just how deeply I had come to trust him, to rely on him.

Darcy's plan unfolded with military precision. He sent out word to his contacts, leveraging his connections and his influence to track down Wickham and Lydia. He dispatched ravens, summoned allies, and even called upon ancient magic to trace the remnants of the spell Wickham had used to spirit Lydia away. I wasn't privy to all the details, but I knew enough to understand that Darcy's resources were vast, his reach extending far beyond anything I could have imagined.

As the hours passed, Darcy remained focused, issuing orders and gathering information. His confidence was reassuring, but beneath it all, I could see the anger simmering just below the surface. This was personal for him—more personal than I had realized.

It wasn't until later that evening, when Darcy pulled me aside, that I began to understand the full extent of Wickham's treachery.

"Elizabeth," he said quietly, his voice low so that no one else could hear. "I have received some troubling information about Wickham's intentions. It appears that he planned this elopement not out of any genuine affection for your sister, but as a means of gaining control over her magic."

I felt my blood run cold at his words. "What do you mean?"

Darcy's expression was grim. "Wickham knew that by taking Lydia, he would place your family in a position of desperation. He intended to use her magic for his own gain, to siphon her power or hold her for ransom. If your family refused his demands… the consequences could be catastrophic."

A wave of nausea washed over me as I realized

just how close we had come to losing everything. Wickham wasn't just a scoundrel—he was a predator, preying on my sister's naivety and our family's vulnerability.

"But why?" I whispered, unable to comprehend such malice. "Why would he do this?"

Darcy's gaze softened, a hint of regret in his eyes. "Wickham is a man driven by greed and resentment. He has no loyalty, no honor. He will do whatever it takes to get what he wants, regardless of who he hurts in the process."

I nodded, my heart heavy with the knowledge that I had been so wrong about everything. Wickham, Darcy, my own judgments—they had all been misguided, tainted by my own prejudices and misconceptions.

But there was no time for self-recrimination. Lydia was still out there, and we had to find her before it was too late.

"Thank you, Fitzwilliam," I said, my voice steady despite the turmoil inside me. "For everything."

He nodded, his expression unreadable. "We will find them, Elizabeth. And when we do, Wickham will face the consequences of his actions."

As Darcy turned to continue his efforts, I felt a sense of resolve settle over me. We would find Lydia.

We had to. And when we did, I would make sure that she understood the gravity of what she had done— and how close she had come to losing not only her own life but her magic and our family's safety as well.

And as I watched Darcy take command of the situation, a new understanding began to take root within me. This man, who had once seemed so distant, so unreachable, was willing to do whatever it took to protect those he cared about. And in that moment, I realized that I was one of them.

For better or worse, I was his. And I knew, with a certainty that shook me to my core, that he would never let anything harm me or my family—not as long as he lived.

14

DARCY

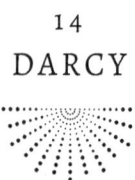

he night was cold and oppressive, the kind that wrapped itself around you, thick and suffocating. The air hung heavy with the scent of damp earth and decay, and the faint rustle of leaves only heightened the tension as I moved stealthily through the underbrush. Each step was measured, every breath controlled, as I approached the abandoned inn that loomed like a dark shadow at the edge of a forgotten village.

The information I had received had led me here, to this desolate place where the magic in the air pulsed with a malevolent energy. Wickham was here, and so was Lydia. But this was no simple rescue mission—this was a battle of wills, of power, of life and death. And I would see it through to the end.

As I neared the inn, I could feel the dark magic that surrounded it, thick and cloying. Wickham's wards were crude but potent, designed to deter all but the most determined. But I was no ordinary intruder. With a whispered incantation, I dispelled the magical defenses, the air shimmering as the barriers crumbled before me.

The door to the inn groaned as I pushed it open, the sound echoing through the eerie silence. Inside, the darkness was nearly absolute, broken only by the faint flicker of candlelight from a room at the far end of a narrow corridor. I moved silently, my senses sharpened, attuned to every movement, every sound. Voices reached my ears—one smooth and oily, the other high-pitched and trembling with fear.

I reached the doorway and paused, my heart pounding with a cold, calculated fury. Wickham stood over Lydia, who was bound to a chair, her face streaked with tears and terror. The sight of her, so frightened and helpless, ignited a rage within me that burned cold and bright.

"Darcy," Wickham sneered as he noticed my presence, his voice dripping with venom. "Always playing the knight in shining armor. How predictable."

I stepped into the room, my gaze never leaving Lydia. "Lydia, come to me," I commanded.

Lydia's eyes widened as she saw me, a flicker of hope in her gaze, but she was too paralyzed by fear to move. Wickham placed a hand on her shoulder, his grip tightening, possessive and cruel.

"She's not going anywhere, Darcy," Wickham spat, his tone laced with malice. "Not unless you want her to pay the price for your interference."

I forced myself to remain calm, though every fiber of my being screamed to tear him apart. "Let her go, Wickham. You've already lost. Don't make this worse for yourself."

Wickham's laugh was low and sinister, sending a chill down my spine. "Lost? Oh no, Darcy. I've only just begun. You see, Lydia and I have plans. She's going to make me a very powerful man. Her magic will ensure that."

My jaw tightened as I fought to keep my anger in check. "Is that what you told her? That you'd marry her, keep her safe?"

For a split second, I saw something flicker in Wickham's eyes—uncertainty, perhaps fear—but it was quickly replaced by cold defiance. "What of it?"

"You and I both know you're lying," I said, my voice dangerously soft. I took a step closer, the air around me crackling with restrained power. "You don't care about Lydia. You only want her magic. And once you've taken what you need, you'll discard her like you do everyone else."

Lydia's eyes widened further, the realization dawning on her as she looked at Wickham with growing horror. "George… is that true?"

Wickham's grip on her shoulder tightened painfully, and his expression twisted with anger. "Don't listen to him, Lydia. He's trying to turn you against me."

But it was too late. The seed of doubt had been planted, and I could see the fear and betrayal in Lydia's eyes as she began to see Wickham for what he truly was. It was all the opening I needed.

Without hesitation, I extended my hand and released a surge of magical energy, a brilliant pulse of light that shot across the room and struck Wickham squarely in the chest. He was thrown backward, his hold on Lydia broken as he slammed into the wall with a grunt of pain.

I unbound her. "Go, Lydia!" I ordered, my voice sharp and unyielding. "Now!"

Lydia stumbled to her feet, her face pale with

fear, but she obeyed. She darted past Wickham, her footsteps echoing through the small, dimly lit room as she fled toward the door.

Wickham recovered quickly, his eyes blazing with fury as he pulled himself to his feet. His hands crackled with dark magic, the air around him shimmering with malevolent energy. "You'll regret that, Darcy," he hissed, his voice a venomous snarl.

But I was ready. Wickham hurled a bolt of dark energy at me, the spell twisting through the air like a living thing. But my shield deflected it easily, the dark magic fizzling out harmlessly as it struck the barrier I had erected around myself.

"You should have killed me when you had the chance," Wickham sneered, his voice laced with bitter hatred. "Now, I'll destroy everything you care about. I'll take Lydia's magic, and then I'll take everything you hold dear."

"I should have," I agreed, my voice cold as ice. "But I won't make that mistake again."

With a swift, precise motion, I unleashed a counterspell, a wave of shimmering light that enveloped Wickham, binding him in place. He struggled against the magical restraints, his expression twisting with rage and desperation as he realized he was outmatched.

"You think you can stop me?" he spat, his voice trembling with fury. "You think you've won?"

"I don't think," I replied, my tone as deadly as the magic I wielded. "I know."

I tightened the magical bonds around him, forcing him to his knees. Wickham gasped, his breath coming in ragged bursts as his power drained away, leaving him weak and defenseless.

"You will leave," I commanded, my voice low and dangerous. "You will leave and never return. If you do, I will end you."

Wickham glared at me, his eyes burning with impotent rage. "This isn't over, Darcy," he hissed, his voice dripping with venom. "I'll find a way. I'll come back, and I'll take everything from you."

"This is over," I said with finality, my voice as cold as the night air. "You're finished."

I released the spell, and Wickham slumped to the ground, his energy spent. He knew he was beaten, and after a moment of hesitation, he scrambled to his feet and fled into the darkness, his footsteps fading into the night.

I stood there for a moment, the adrenaline still coursing through my veins, the taste of victory tinged with bitterness. This was not the end of Wickham—not yet. But it was a start.

Turning on my heel, I hurried after Lydia. I found her huddled near the carriage, trembling with fear and relief. When she saw me, she burst into tears, her sobs wracking her small frame.

"Lydia," I said softly, my voice gentler now as I approached her. "It's over. You're safe."

She looked up at me, her eyes filled with gratitude and shame. "I'm so sorry, Mr. Darcy. I didn't know... I didn't know what he really was."

"It's not your fault," I replied, helping her into the carriage. "Wickham is a master of deception. He preys on those who trust him. But he won't hurt you again. I'll make sure of that."

As the carriage set off back to Longbourn Hollow, I sat beside Lydia, my mind already turning to the steps I would take to ensure her safety and protect Elizabeth's family from any further harm. Wickham had shown his true colors, and I would see to it that he paid for his treachery.

When we arrived at Longbourn Hollow, I escorted Lydia inside and spoke with Mr. Bennet, who was overcome with relief but also deeply concerned about the potential fallout from Lydia's actions. I assured him that the matter would be handled discreetly, that Lydia's magic would be protected, and that Wickham would not be able to use her or her powers for his own gain.

It was then that I made the decision to pay off Wickham's debts, to ensure he would not return to torment the Bennet family. It was a significant sum, but one I was willing to part with if it meant protecting Elizabeth and her family from further harm.

As I stood outside Longbourn Hollow, watching the first light of dawn creep over the horizon, a strange sense of peace settled over me. I had done what was necessary—not for recognition or thanks, but because it was the right thing to do.

And because, deep down, I knew that I would do anything to protect Elizabeth Bennet and the people she cared about.

As I turned to leave, I cast one last glance at the house, a bittersweet smile tugging at my lips. I knew that Elizabeth might never know the extent of what I had done, and that was as it should be. This was not about earning her favor—it was about doing what was right.

15

ELIZABETH

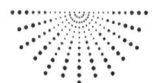

*T*he news of Lydia's return spread quickly through Longbourn Hollow, bringing with it a wave of relief that washed over our family. The dark cloud of scandal that had loomed so ominously now seemed to dissipate, leaving behind only the faint echoes of the storm. But as the initial shock and fear began to fade, a new set of emotions took their place—gratitude, confusion, and something else I couldn't quite name.

I had seen Darcy only briefly when he brought Lydia back to us, ensuring her safe return before leaving with little more than a few curt words. But the memory of that moment haunted me, the way his presence had filled the room, commanding and unyielding, yet somehow tinged with a raw, unspoken intensity. The way his eyes had met mine for just a fraction of a second, sending a jolt of electricity through my veins.

I couldn't stop thinking about him, about the way he had stepped in to save my sister, to save my family. He had taken charge with a ferocity that was both terrifying and exhilarating, and the way he had looked at me before leaving had left me breathless with a need I couldn't quite define.

Later that day, I found myself pacing the floor of my room, unable to shake the memory of that brief encounter. The air between us had been charged with something potent, something that made my heart race and my skin tingle with anticipation. I knew I needed to speak to him, to understand why he had done what he did, and to tell him how grateful I was.

But more than that, I wanted to be near him, to feel that intensity again, to lose myself in the fire that burned between us.

With a resolute breath, I made my way to my father's study, knowing he would be eager to hear the details of Lydia's return. But when I entered the room, I was the one who delivered the news.

"Papa," I began, my voice steady but filled with

emotion, "it was Mr. Darcy who brought Lydia back to us."

My father looked up, surprise flickering in his eyes. "Darcy? He did this?"

I nodded, the words tumbling out of me in a rush. "Yes. He found her, confronted Wickham, and ensured she was returned safely. He paid off Wickham's debts to ensure our family's reputation would be protected. He did it all... for us."

My father's expression softened, and he leaned back in his chair, clearly moved by the revelation. "I misjudged that man, Lizzy. I never would have thought him capable of such generosity."

Neither would I, I thought, though the realization had been slowly dawning on me ever since Darcy had left our house. But there was something more to this, something that went beyond mere gratitude. There was a need in me, a longing that I had tried to ignore, but it had only grown stronger with each passing hour.

As evening fell, I found myself wandering outside, the cool air doing little to calm the storm of emotions inside me. I was lost in thought when I heard footsteps approaching, and I turned to see Darcy standing there, his eyes locked onto mine with that same fierce intensity.

"Miss Bennet," he said, his voice low and commanding, sending a shiver down my spine. "We need to talk."

I swallowed, trying to steady my racing heart. "Yes, Mr. Darcy. We do."

He stepped closer, his presence overwhelming, and I could feel the heat radiating off him, a tangible force that made my pulse quicken. "Lydia is safe now," he said, his voice a growl that sent a thrill through me. "But make no mistake, Elizabeth, I will not allow Wickham to harm you or your family again. He deserves no mercy, and I will make sure he gets none."

His words were laced with a dark promise, and I felt a surge of desire unlike anything I had ever known. The way he spoke, the way he looked at me —it was as if he was claiming me, asserting his dominance in a way that made my knees weak with longing.

"And what about me, Mr. Darcy?" I asked, my voice trembling with both fear and excitement. "What do you intend to do with me?"

He stepped even closer, his eyes burning with an intensity that took my breath away. "You are mine, Elizabeth," he said, his voice rough with emotion. "I will do whatever it takes to protect you, to keep you safe. And that means ensuring that all your needs are met."

The implication in his words sent a rush of heat through me, and I felt myself growing wet with need, my body responding to him in ways I had never experienced before.

"Is that so?" I challenged, trying to maintain some semblance of control even as I felt it slipping away. "And what if I don't need your protection, Mr. Darcy?"

His eyes darkened, and he reached out, his hand sliding around the back of my neck, pulling me closer until our bodies were almost touching. "You may not think you need it, Elizabeth," he murmured, his lips brushing against my ear, "but I assure you, you do. And I intend to provide it… in every way you could possibly imagine."

The raw power in his words made me shudder with desire, and I found myself leaning into him, craving his touch, his dominance. The heat between us was unbearable, the tension so thick it was suffocating.

But before I could respond, before I could give in to the need that was threatening to consume me, Darcy released me, stepping back with a controlled grace that only made me want him more.

"I have loose ends to tie up," he said, his voice regaining some of its composure. "But when I return, Elizabeth, we will continue this conversation. And when we do, you will find that I am a man of my word."

His eyes met mine one last time, and the promise in them was clear. He was going to take me, claim me, in every way possible. And I was going to let him.

As he turned and walked away, I stood there, my body trembling with a need that was as exhilarating as it was terrifying. Darcy was unlike any man I had ever known, and the fire he had ignited in me was one that I knew would never be extinguished.

I was his. Completely and utterly.

16

ELIZABETH

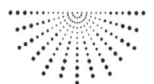

The arrival of Lady Catherine de Bourgh in Longbourn Hollow was as sudden as it was unnerving. Her grand carriage, drawn by sleek black horses with eyes that seemed to glow with an unnatural light, rolled up to Longbourn with an imposing presence that sent ripples of unease through the village. I had heard whispers of Lady Catherine, but I had never met her. Her reputation as a formidable sorceress preceded her, though the stories were vague and filled with speculation.

When the housemaid informed me that a certain Lady Catherine wished to speak with me privately, my heart sank with foreboding. The name rang a bell, but I couldn't place it immediately. It wasn't until I entered the drawing room and saw the tall, imposing figure before me that I realized exactly who she was.

Lady Catherine de Bourgh.

Her entrance was nothing short of theatrical. She swept into the room with an air of authority that brooked no opposition, her posture rigid and her eyes as sharp as daggers. She was a tall woman, her presence commanding, and she carried herself with the kind of confidence that comes from years of being obeyed without question. Her dark, heavy gown rustled like the wings of a raven, and the faint scent of incense clung to her, adding to the aura of mystique that surrounded her.

"Miss Bennet," she began, her voice cold and commanding, cutting through the air with a tone that left no room for pleasantries. "I trust you are aware of who I am?"

I inclined my head slightly, keeping my tone polite but firm. "I have heard of you, Lady Catherine, though we have never been introduced."

Her eyes narrowed, and she took a step closer, the intensity of her gaze making the air around her seem to crackle with restrained power. "Then allow me to enlighten you. I am Lady Catherine de Bourgh, and I have come here to discuss a matter of grave importance that concerns my nephew, Fitzwilliam Darcy."

At the mention of Darcy's name, my heart skipped a beat, but I maintained my composure. "What matter would that be, Lady Catherine?"

Her lips curled into a thin, humorless smile, and she eyed me as if assessing an opponent. "There are disturbing rumors, Miss Bennet—rumors that you have ensnared my nephew with your charms. I have come to put an end to these rumors and to ensure that you understand the gravity of the situation."

The accusation hung in the air between us, sharp and pointed, but I refused to be intimidated. "I'm afraid I don't understand, Lady Catherine. What exactly are you accusing me of?"

She drew herself up to her full height, her gaze cold and unyielding. "You come from a family of little magical prowess and even less consequence. You have neither wealth nor connections to recommend you, and the idea that you could ever be a suitable match for my nephew is absurd. I am here to make it abundantly clear that any connection between you and Mr. Darcy must end immediately."

Her words struck a chord of anger within me, but I forced myself to remain calm. "And what if Mr. Darcy does not share your views, Lady Catherine?

What if he has made his own decisions about his future?"

Lady Catherine's eyes flashed with indignation, and the air around her seemed to pulse with a dark energy. "Mr. Darcy's future has been decided since his birth. He is to marry my daughter, Anne de Bourgh, in a union that will strengthen both of our magical bloodlines and ensure the continuation of our legacy. You, Miss Bennet, are nothing more than an obstacle in the way of that plan."

Her words were meant to frighten me, to force me into submission, but they only served to ignite a spark of defiance deep within me. I had spent too long letting others dictate my life, letting their expectations and prejudices shape my decisions. This was my future, my heart, and I would not be bullied into submission by anyone, not even a powerful sorceress like Lady Catherine.

"Lady Catherine," I said, my voice steady and unwavering, "I respect your position, but I will not be intimidated by it. Mr. Darcy is a man of his own mind, and it is for him to decide whom he wishes to marry, not you."

Her expression darkened, and the temperature in the room seemed to drop. "You are a foolish girl, Miss Bennet. Do you think you can defy me and come away unscathed? I have the power to strip you and your family of what little standing you have, to ensure that you are cast out of the magical community and forgotten. Do not test my patience."

"I am not testing your patience, Lady Catherine," I replied, meeting her gaze without flinching. "I am simply standing up for my right to choose my own future. If Mr. Darcy wishes to marry Miss de Bourgh, that is his choice. But if he does not, then you have no right to force him into a union he does not desire."

The tension between us crackled with magical energy, and for a moment, the room was silent. Lady Catherine's eyes bore into mine, searching for any sign of weakness, but I refused to back down. This was a battle I had not chosen, but one I was determined to fight.

Finally, Lady Catherine let out a huff of exasperation, her composure slipping just enough to reveal the frustration beneath. "You are as stubborn as you are foolish, Miss Bennet. But mark my words—you will regret this. You will regret ever daring to think you could usurp my plans for my nephew."

With that, she turned on her heel and swept out of the room, her skirts rustling like the wings of a stormcloud. The door closed behind her with a decisive thud, leaving me standing there, my heart pounding in my chest.

For a moment, I could hardly believe what had just happened. Lady Catherine's ultimatum, her threats and accusations, had shaken me, but they had also solidified something within me—something that had been growing ever since Darcy had come into my life and that had only strengthened with each passing day.

I loved him.

The realization hit me with a force that took my breath away. I loved Fitzwilliam Darcy, not despite his flaws, but because of them. I loved the man who had gone to such lengths to protect my family, the man who had shown me kindness and under-standing even when I had not deserved it. I loved the man who had the courage to defy the expectations of others and follow his own heart.

And I would not let Lady Catherine, or anyone else, take that away from me.

I felt a new resolve settle over me, a sense of purpose that banished the lingering doubts and fears. Lady Catherine's threats no longer held any power over me because I knew what I wanted, and I was willing to fight for it.

I would find Darcy, and I would tell him the truth

—about my feelings, about the change in my heart, and about the future I wanted to build with him. It would not be easy, and there would be obstacles to overcome, but I was ready to face them, whatever they might be.

With a deep breath, I left the drawing room and made my way to the garden, where I could gather my thoughts and prepare for what lay ahead. The path before me was uncertain, but I knew one thing with absolute clarity: I would follow my heart, wherever it might lead. And I would do so with the strength and courage that Darcy himself had shown me.

17

DARCY

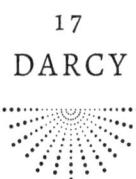

I stood by the window of my study at Netherfield, gazing out at the tranquil landscape, my thoughts far from the serenity of the scene before me.

Elizabeth Bennet.

Her name echoed in my mind like a persistent refrain, refusing to be silenced. I had tried, in vain, to focus on other matters, to distract myself with the affairs of the estate, with the endless correspondence that required my attention. But no matter how hard I tried, my thoughts always returned to her.

Elizabeth, with her sharp wit and even sharper tongue. Elizabeth, who had challenged me in ways no one else ever had. Elizabeth, who had made me question everything I thought I knew about myself and the world around me.

I had spent so much time wrestling with my feelings for her, trying to push them aside, to convince myself that they were impractical, impossible. But the more I tried to deny them, the stronger they became, until they were an undeniable force, pulling me toward her with an intensity I could no longer ignore.

I loved her.

The realization was both terrifying and exhilarating, filling me with a sense of urgency that I could not escape. I loved Elizabeth Bennet, and I could not imagine a future without her by my side.

My decision was made. I would go to her, and I would tell her the truth. I would lay my heart bare before her, and whatever the outcome, I would accept it. But I had to try. I had to let her know how deeply I cared for her, how much she had come to mean to me.

With a renewed sense of purpose, I left the study and prepared myself for the journey to Longbourn. But this was not a journey to be taken on foot or by carriage—no, the urgency in my heart called for something swifter, something magical. With a murmured incantation, I called forth the winds, and a shimmering portal began to form before me, swirling with the colors of the setting sun.

Stepping through the portal, I found myself instantly transported to the edge of Longbourn's garden, where the fading light of the day cast long shadows across the neatly trimmed hedges. The air was thick with the scent of blooming flowers and the subtle hum of lingering magic, a reminder of the ancient spells that had been woven into the very fabric of this place.

I hesitated for a moment, feeling the weight of the magic that surrounded me, a magic that had been part of Elizabeth's life long before I entered it. This was her world, and I was an intruder, an outsider who had only just begun to understand the depth and beauty of it.

But then I saw her—Elizabeth, standing by a bed of roses, her back to me as she gazed out at the setting sun. She looked peaceful, contemplative, and the sight of her filled me with a warmth that spread through my chest, dispelling any lingering doubts.

For a moment, I simply watched her, marveling at the way the golden light played across her features, casting her in a soft, almost ethereal glow. She was beautiful—more beautiful than I had ever allowed myself to admit—and the thought of losing her, of never being able to tell her how I truly felt, was unbearable.

Taking a deep breath, I stepped forward, the portal closing silently behind me as I moved toward her. The soft rustle of leaves was the only sound as I approached, and then she turned, her eyes meeting mine, and the uncertainty melted away.

"Mr. Darcy," she said, her voice soft but steady. "I wasn't expecting you."

I took a deep breath, gathering my courage. "Elizabeth, I hope you don't mind my intrusion. There is something I must say to you."

She looked at me with apprehension, and I could see the flicker of emotions in her eyes, emotions that I desperately hoped would mirror my own.

"Please, go on," she said, her voice barely above a whisper.

I stepped closer, my heart racing as I spoke. "Elizabeth, from the moment I met you, I was captivated by your wit, your spirit, your intelligence. You challenged me in ways no one else ever has, and though I fought against it, my feelings for you grew stronger with each passing day."

I paused, searching her face for any sign of how she might respond. "I know that I have made mistakes—many mistakes. But I need you to know that my feelings for you have never wavered. I love you, Elizabeth. I love you more than words can express, and I am willing to face any challenge, any obstacle, if it means I can be with you."

The words hung in the air between us, the weight of them pressing down on my chest as I waited, breathless, for her response.

For a moment, Elizabeth said nothing, her expression unreadable. My heart clenched with fear —had I been too late? Had I misjudged her feelings once again?

But then, slowly, a soft smile spread across her lips, and her eyes filled with a warmth that took my breath away.

"Oh, Mr. Darcy," she began, her voice trembling slightly. "You cannot know how much your words mean to me. I must confess that I, too, have made mistakes." She took a step closer, her gaze never leaving mine. "I love you, too. I love you more than I ever thought possible, and I cannot imagine a future without you."

The relief, the joy that surged through me at her words was overwhelming. I felt as if a great weight had been lifted from my shoulders, and I could hardly believe that this moment—this perfect, beautiful moment—was real.

"Elizabeth," I whispered. "You have made me the happiest man in the world."

She smiled, her eyes shining with unshed tears. "And you, Mr. Darcy, have made me the happiest woman."

I reached out, gently taking her hand in mine, and felt the familiar surge of magical energy that always accompanied our touch, a connection between us so powerful, so undeniable, that it felt as if the world had shifted beneath our feet. We stood there, in the fading light of the day, holding onto each other as if we were the only two people in the world.

In that moment, all the misunderstandings, the obstacles, the pain—they all melted away, leaving only the love we felt for one another, a love that had been hard-won, but all the more precious for it.

I pulled Elizabeth into my arms, the restraint I had so carefully maintained beginning to fray at the edges. The feel of her body pressed against mine, the warmth of her breath on my neck—it ignited a fire within me that I could no longer ignore.

But even as I held her, a part of me was acutely aware of the fragility of the moment. This was the woman I loved—the woman who had unwittingly challenged every principle I held dear. She had made me question my own beliefs, had made me confront the darker parts of myself that I had long tried to bury. And now, here she was, in my arms, trusting me with her heart.

I pulled back slightly, just enough to look into her eyes, and what I saw there nearly undid me. There was love, yes, but also desire—a mirrored reflection of the need that was roaring through my veins.

"Elizabeth," I whispered, my voice rough need.

Her eyes widened slightly. "I need you too."

That was all the permission I required.

With a low growl, I captured her lips with mine, the kiss fierce and possessive, a stark contrast to the gentle way I had held her only moments before. My hands moved to her waist, pulling her closer, and I felt her body yield to mine, her soft curves pressing against the hard planes of my chest.

The world around us disappeared, leaving only the two of us locked in this moment of raw, unbridled passion. I could feel her heart racing against mine, the rapid thrum of her pulse matching the wild beat of my own. It was intoxicating, the way she responded to my touch, her fingers tangling in my hair as she returned the kiss with equal fervor.

I backed her against the wall, the solid surface

JAX WILDER

grounding me as I lost myself in the heat of her mouth, the taste of her driving me to the edge of reason. My hands roamed over her body, exploring the delicate curves, the softness of her skin, the places that made her shiver and gasp with pleasure.

"Elizabeth," I groaned against her lips. "I need you... I need all of you."

She responded with a breathless moan, her hands gripping my shoulders as if to anchor herself to me. "Fitzwilliam... please..."

Her plea undid the last thread of my restraint. I pushed her harder against the wall, my hands moving with a sense of urgency as I claimed her lips once more, my kiss deep and demanding. I wanted to possess her, to mark her as mine in every possible way, to show her the depths of the passion I had kept hidden for so long.

My hands slid down to her thighs, lifting her effortlessly as I pressed her against the wall, her legs wrapping around my waist in a way that made me shudder with need. I could feel the heat of her body against mine, the evidence of her own desire stoking the flames of my own.

"Tell me you're mine," I demanded.

"I'm yours," she whispered, her voice shaky but filled with a certainty that made my heart swell with

164

possessive pride. "I'm yours, Fitzwilliam. I've always been yours."

The sound of her surrender, the way she offered herself to me so completely. I had never wanted anything or anyone as much as I wanted her in this moment.

But as much as I wanted to lose myself in her, to let go of all control and take what we both so desperately needed, I knew there was more I needed to express—something even deeper than the physical connection we were about to share.

With a guttural groan, I forced myself to pull back slightly, my breath coming in ragged gasps as I tried to regain some semblance of control. I could see the confusion and disappointment in her eyes, the flush of desire still evident on her cheeks, and it nearly broke me.

"Elizabeth," I whispered, my voice hoarse with emotion. "I need you to understand… this isn't just about passion. This is about forever. I want you to be mine, not just for tonight, but for every night, for every day that we're granted together."

Her eyes softened, and she nodded, her hands gently caressing my face as she spoke. "I know, Fitzwilliam. I want that too. I want all of it."

The certainty in her words was all the encouragement I needed. With a renewed sense of purpose, I captured her lips once more, my kiss slower this time, more deliberate, as if sealing the promise we had just made to each other.

The moment Elizabeth stood before me, I felt the surge of possessive hunger that had been simmering beneath the surface. She was mine—completely and utterly mine—and I would make sure she knew it.

"Undress for me, Elizabeth," I commanded, my voice low and firm, leaving no room for hesitation.

Her breath caught, but she obeyed, her hands trembling slightly as she reached for the buttons of her dress. She undid them slowly, deliberately, her eyes never leaving mine. The fabric slipped from her shoulders, revealing the smooth, pale skin of her collarbone, then her perfect breasts. The sight of her, so vulnerable yet so willing, made my cock strain painfully against my trousers.

I shifted, adjusting myself as the desire became nearly unbearable. Elizabeth noticed, and her eyes flashed with wicked amusement. She let the dress fall to the floor, leaving her in nothing but the barest of undergarments. My voice was a growl, deep and rough with need.

"Touch your pussy, Elizabeth," I ordered, the command laced with dark desire.

She hesitated, her cheeks flushing a deep crimson. "I've never... done that," she stammered, her voice barely above a whisper.

My eyes narrowed, both surprised and challenged. "Not even after I tasted you? After I made you come?" The words were meant to push her, to break through the last of her resistance.

Elizabeth's blush deepened, and she looked down, struggling to find the words. "N-no..."

A low tsk escaped my lips, disappointment washing over me. "That's disappointing, Lizzy. You lied to me. Why would you do that?" I asked, watching her intently, waiting for her to answer.

She shrugged playfully, swaying her hips back and forth, teasing me with the motion. "Maybe I wanted to see how far you'd go to punish me," she replied, her voice a sultry whisper.

"Come here," I commanded, my tone leaving no room for defiance.

She stepped closer, her movements slow and deliberate. I sat down on the nearest couch, my eyes never leaving hers as I patted my lap. "You need to be punished for lying, Elizabeth. Good girls don't lie to their lords."

She pouted, covering herself with her hands in a playful act of defiance. My gaze darkened, my voice a low growl as I reprimanded her. "I didn't tell you to cover yourself. I'm going to have to punish you for that too."

She bit her lip, her eyes sparkling with mischief as she looked up at me. "But what if I want to taste you, my lord?" she asked, her voice dripping with temptation.

"Not before I punish you," I responded, my voice firm, unyielding.

Without warning, I grabbed her by the waist, pulling her down onto my lap with a force that made her gasp. I laid her naked body across my knees, her ass up and perfectly positioned for my hand. Her legs dangled off the edge of the couch, her heart pounding in anticipation—I could feel it in the way she trembled against me.

I rubbed her exposed buttocks, my touch both gentle and possessive. "You're soft in all the right places," I murmured, feeling her shiver beneath my hands. "I'm going to make you come, but first, you need to learn your lesson."

I pulled my hand back and brought it down sharply on her ass, the sound of the smack echoing in the quiet room. Elizabeth moaned, the sting of the slap mingling with the pleasure that I knew was shooting through her. I kept my hand on the spot, rubbing the heated skin as I spoke. "Are you going to lie to me again?"

She didn't answer right away, her breath coming in short, sharp gasps. I delivered another smack, my hand coming down on the opposite cheek. She squirmed beneath me, her moans growing louder as she writhed in pleasure.

"Are you going to lie to me again?" I asked, my voice a low growl.

"No, my lord," Elizabeth whimpered, her voice trembling with submission. "I won't lie to you again."

"Good girl," I praised, my hand sliding down between her legs, finding her slick with heat. "Have you touched your pussy before?"

Elizabeth hesitated, her breath catching in her throat. I stilled my hand, then delivered another sharp smack, this time slipping a finger inside her. She lurched forward, a cry of pleasure escaping her lips.

"I said," my voice was a dangerous whisper, "have you touched yourself before?"

She nodded, her words coming out in a breathless moan. "Yes... yes, I have."

A smirk tugged at the corners of my mouth as I continued exploring her slick folds. I added a second finger, stretching her as I moved in and out of her, teasing her clit with every glide. "Have you tasted your sweet cunt before, Lizzy?" I asked, my tone both commanding and seductive.

She shook her head, too consumed by the pleasure to speak.

I pulled my fingers out of her, helping her upright. Holding my fingers up, I brought them to my nose, inhaling her scent before licking up one side. Then, I held them out to her. "Taste yourself," I ordered.

Elizabeth took my fingers into her mouth, sucking and licking them clean with a sinful smile. The sight of her, so willing, so eager to please, made my cock throb painfully.

"You're so wet," I murmured, my voice thick with desire. "Dripping with juices. You need a good fucking, don't you, baby?"

She nodded, whimpering with need.

I stood, undressing quickly, my cock hard and ready, straining toward her. Elizabeth watched in fascination as I stroked myself once, her eyes wide with anticipation. She reached out, tugging me closer until I was standing before her, my cock at her mouth level.

She licked her lips before placing a soft kiss on

the tip. "Oh, it's so soft," she murmured in surprise, her tongue darting out to lick along my shaft.

I groaned, my control slipping further as she continued to explore me with her mouth. But the need to be inside her, to claim her completely, was too overwhelming. I couldn't wait any longer.

With a rough movement, I laid her back on the couch, my hands gripping her hips as I positioned myself at her entrance. I thrust into her with one powerful stroke, filling her completely. Elizabeth cried out in pleasure, her body arching against me as I stretched her, filling every inch of her.

"So fucking tight," I groaned, pulling out only to thrust back in, the sensation of her heat nearly sending me over the edge.

I took one of her breasts into my mouth, my tongue playing with her nipple as I thrust into her again and again, each movement pushing her closer to the edge. Elizabeth panted, her body trembling with the intensity of the pleasure I was giving her.

I slipped a hand between us, finding the nub between her pussy lips, rubbing it in time with my thrusts. Elizabeth's moans grew louder, her body tightening around my cock as the pleasure built to an unbearable peak.

"I'm almost... almost..." she gasped, her voice trembling with need.

"Come for me, Elizabeth," I growled, my voice thick with my own impending release. "Scream my name when you come."

With a final, powerful thrust, Elizabeth screamed my name as she came, her body convulsing with the force of her orgasm. The sensation of her pussy tightening around my cock sent me over the edge, and with a groan, I spilled my seed deep inside her, filling her with my release.

As we both came down from the high, I remained inside her, my body still trembling with the aftershocks of my climax. I leaned down, pressing a soft kiss to her lips, my heart swelling with the realization of how much I wanted this woman—how much I needed her in my life.

"I love you, Elizabeth," I whispered against her skin, my voice filled with a quiet intensity. "And I'm never letting you go."

With those words, I sealed our fate, knowing that I had found in Elizabeth not just a lover, but a partner, an equal, and the woman who would forever be mine.

For a long moment, we simply lay there, our bodies entwined, our breaths mingling as we came down from the heights of our passion. The room was filled with the sound of our ragged breathing, the rapid beating of our hearts, and the faint crackle of magic that seemed to hum in the air around us.

It was only when the last echoes of our shared pleasure had faded that I remembered the other reason I had come to Elizabeth tonight. With trembling fingers, I reached into the pocket of my discarded coat and pulled out the small velvet box that had been hidden there.

"Elizabeth," I murmured, my voice hoarse with the lingering effects of our passion. "There's something I need to ask you."

She looked up at me, her eyes still hazy with the afterglow of our lovemaking, but filled with curiosity. "What is it, Fitzwilliam?"

I took a deep breath, my heart pounding in my chest as I opened the box to reveal the ring nestled inside. It was a simple band, set with a single, brilliant diamond that sparkled in the dim light of the room—a symbol of the love I felt for her, a love that was pure and unbreakable.

"Elizabeth Bennet," I said, my voice steady despite the tumult of emotions swirling within me, "will you marry me? Will you be mine forever, in every way?"

For a moment, there was only silence, the world seeming to hold its breath as I waited for her answer. And then, slowly, a radiant smile spread across her lips, and her eyes filled with tears of joy.

"Yes, Fitzwilliam," she whispered, her voice trembling with emotion. "Yes, I will marry you. I will be yours, forever."

The relief, the joy that surged through me at her words was overwhelming, and I felt as if a great weight had been lifted from my shoulders. With a smile that mirrored her own, I slipped the ring onto her finger, a perfect fit, just as we were for each other.

I pulled her into my arms. I was Fitzwilliam Darcy, and she was Elizabeth Bennet.

And we were bound by a love that was stronger than any force in the world.

18

ELIZABETH

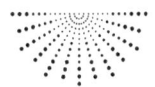

The days following Darcy's declaration of love felt like a dream—one so vivid and beautiful that I half expected to wake up and find it all a figment of my imagination. But every time I looked into his eyes, every time his hand found mine, I knew it was real. We had found each other despite the misunderstandings, the magic that had once seemed to divide us, and the obstacles that had threatened to keep us apart. Now, as we stood on the cusp of a new future, the world seemed full of possibilities.

Our engagement was announced with little fanfare, as both Darcy and I preferred to keep the news private at first, sharing it only with our closest family members. My mother's reaction was, predictably, one of astonishment and delight.

"Lizzie, my dear Lizzie, I always knew you would make a fine match!" she exclaimed, her eyes wide with excitement. "Mr. Darcy! Who would have thought? You must have enchanted him completely!"

I smiled at her enthusiasm, knowing that it was our love and not any spell that had brought us together. Our journey to this moment had been anything but straightforward, and yet that made our bond all the more precious.

My father's reaction was more subdued, but no less heartfelt. He took me aside one evening, his usually reserved expression softened by a rare display of emotion.

"Lizzie," he began, his voice gentle, "I must admit that I never imagined you would choose a man like Darcy. But having seen how he has acted—how he has gone out of his way to protect our family, and how deeply he cares for you—I can see that you have made the right choice. I am proud of you, my dear."

His words brought tears to my eyes, and I hugged him tightly, grateful for his understanding and support.

Jane, as always, was my constant confidante. She listened with a kind and open heart as I told her about everything that had happened, from Lady Catherine's ultimatum to Darcy's proposal. Her joy for me was boundless, and she shared in my happiness as if it were her own.

One afternoon, as Darcy and I strolled through the garden, we were surprised by the arrival of none other than Mr. Bingley. He approached us with a broad smile, his eyes alight with excitement.

"Miss Bennet," he began, his voice full of warmth, "I have come to ask for Jane's hand in marriage. I cannot wait another moment to make her my wife."

Darcy and I exchanged a glance, both of us smiling at Bingley's eagerness. "Jane is inside, Mr. Bingley," I said, my voice full of encouragement. "I'm sure she will be overjoyed to see you."

Bingley nodded gratefully and hurried into the house, his heart set on securing the future he had always wanted with Jane. Darcy and I continued our walk, both of us knowing that this day would mark a new beginning not just for us, but for Jane and Bingley as well.

Later that evening, Jane sought me out, her cheeks flushed and her eyes shining with a joy that made my heart swell with happiness for her.

"Lizzie," she said, her voice trembling with excitement, "Charles proposed! He was so sincere, so full of love... I said yes, of course. We're going to be married!"

I embraced her, my heart overflowing with love and pride for my sister. "Oh, Jane, I am so happy for you. You and Mr. Bingley are perfect for each other."

Her smile was radiant, and I knew that whatever challenges lay ahead, Jane and Bingley would face them together, just as Darcy and I would.

As the days passed, the news of our engagements began to spread throughout Longbourn Hollow. The reactions were overwhelmingly positive, with friends and neighbors expressing their happiness and well-wishes for both couples. The village, which had always been close-knit, seemed to embrace our unions as a cause for celebration.

Darcy, who had once been viewed as aloof and unapproachable, began to show a different side of himself to the townspeople. He took an active interest in the community, using his influence to support local businesses and improve the lives of those around him. His efforts did not go unnoticed, and slowly but surely, the people of Longbourn Hollow began to accept him—not just as an outsider, but as one of their own.

The transformation was not just social but magical as well. Darcy and I found ourselves working together to protect the magical harmony of the village, a task that required both of our unique gifts. The ancient wards that had once protected Longbourn Hollow from dark forces were weakening, and together, Darcy and I reinforced them with a blend of his powerful, disciplined magic and my more intuitive, nature-based spells. The villagers, who had always felt the presence of these protective charms without fully understanding them, began to see us as their guardians, a role we embraced with a shared sense of purpose.

As for me, I found myself growing more confident in my new role, not as the wife of a wealthy and powerful man, but as an equal partner in our relationship. Darcy and I made plans for our future together, discussing everything from the management of our estates to the simple pleasures of everyday life. We spoke of travel, of exploring the world together, but we also cherished the idea of a quiet life at Pemberley, surrounded by the beauty of the countryside.

The acceptance of our unions by the townspeople culminated in a celebration—a gathering in the village square where everyone came together to share in our happiness. There were flowers and music, laughter and dancing, and as Darcy and I stood hand in hand, watching the festivities, I felt a deep sense of contentment.

This was the beginning of a new chapter, not just for us, but for everyone whose lives had been touched by our journey. The misunderstandings, the pride, and the prejudices that had once kept us apart had been overcome, leaving behind only the love that had brought us together.

As the sun set on that joyful day, casting a warm, golden glow over the village, Darcy turned to me, his eyes filled with a tenderness that made my heart swell.

"Elizabeth," he said softly, "I never imagined that I could be this happy. You have given me so much—more than I ever thought possible."

I smiled, my heart full. "And you, Mr. Darcy, have shown me that true love is worth fighting for. I am so grateful that we found our way to each other."

He lifted my hand to his lips, pressing a gentle kiss to my fingers. "Our future together, Elizabeth, will be filled with all the happiness and adventure we could ever dream of. I promise you that."

As I looked into his eyes, I knew that no matter what challenges we might face, we would face them together. Our love, tested and true, would carry us through whatever the future held.

And so, as we stood there, surrounded by the warmth and joy of our friends and family, I knew that this was only the beginning of our story—a story of love, resilience, and the unbreakable bond that had brought us together.

It was, truly, a new beginning, and one that we would embrace with all the magic and love in our hearts.

19
DARCY

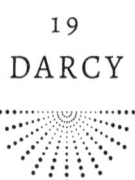

The night was eerily still, a thick fog rolling in from the moors that seemed to swallow the world in a blanket of silence. I stood by the window of our home, Pemberley, gazing out into the darkness, a sense of unease settling over me like a shroud. Something was coming—something I could not yet see but could feel in the marrow of my bones.

Elizabeth was beside me, her presence a steadying force that grounded me even as the ominous tension in the air grew thicker. We had been through so much together, overcome so many obstacles, but this felt different. This felt like a final reckoning.

"Do you sense it?" Elizabeth asked quietly, her voice tinged with the same apprehension I felt.

I nodded, my gaze still fixed on the fog-shrouded landscape. "Yes. Something is wrong. I can feel it."

She reached out and took my hand, her touch warm and reassuring despite the cold dread that had settled in my chest. "Whatever it is, we will face it together."

Her words, simple yet profound, filled me with a renewed sense of determination. We had faced down danger before—Wickham's treachery, Lady Catherine's threats—and we had emerged stronger for it. But now, it seemed that our greatest challenge was upon us.

As if summoned by our thoughts, a shadowy figure emerged from the fog, moving slowly but purposefully toward Pemberley. Even from this distance, I recognized the figure's gait, the unmistakable aura of malevolence that surrounded him.

Wickham.

The sight of him, once a friend and now an enemy consumed by hatred, filled me with a cold fury. He had returned, and I knew without a doubt that he intended to finish what he had started.

"I will not let him harm you," I vowed, my voice low and fierce. "Not now, not ever."

Elizabeth's grip on my hand tightened, and she met my gaze with a fierce resolve of her own. "And I will not let him tear us apart. We are stronger together, Darcy. He has no power over us."

We both knew that Wickham was more dangerous than ever. Rumors had reached us that he had been delving into forbidden dark magic, seeking out powers that were long thought to be lost or too dangerous to wield. His desperation had driven him to madness, and now he had returned to Longbourn Hollow with one goal: to destroy us.

As Wickham drew closer, I could feel the dark energy radiating off him, like a noxious cloud that tainted everything in its path. But Elizabeth was right—we were stronger together. Our love, our bond, was a force that Wickham could never understand or conquer.

I turned to Elizabeth, my voice steady. "We must be prepared. He will not fight fair, and his magic will be strong."

She nodded, her expression resolute. "But our magic is stronger. Because it is born of love, not hate."

Together, we stepped out into the night, leaving the warmth and safety of Pemberley behind. The air crackled with tension, the fog swirling around us like a living thing, but we stood firm, side by side, ready to face whatever Wickham had in store.

As he approached, his face twisted into a cruel smile, the dark magic that clung to him like a second skin pulsing with malevolent energy. "Darcy," he sneered, his voice dripping with contempt. "And Elizabeth. How touching, to see you standing together. But it won't save you."

"You've already lost, Wickham," I replied, my voice cold and unyielding. "There is nothing you can do to harm us now."

Wickham's eyes narrowed, and he raised his hands, dark tendrils of magic swirling around his fingers. "We'll see about that."

Without warning, he unleashed a bolt of dark energy, aimed directly at Elizabeth. But I was faster. Drawing on my own magic, I threw up a barrier, the force of the impact sending a shockwave through the ground but leaving us unharmed.

Elizabeth didn't hesitate. With a swift motion, she called upon her own magic, sending a wave of light cascading toward Wickham. He recoiled, momentarily blinded by the purity of her power, but quickly regained his footing, his rage intensifying.

"You think your love will protect you?" he spat, his voice laced with venom. "You're fools! Love is weak! It's nothing compared to the power I've gained!"

But even as he spoke, I could see the cracks in his facade. His magic, though powerful, was unstable, wild, and chaotic. It was a reflection of the darkness that had consumed him, and it would be his undoing.

"We are not fools, Wickham," Elizabeth replied, her voice calm and strong. "We are stronger because we fight for each other, not for ourselves."

With those words, we unleashed our combined magic, a force born of love, respect, and a deep connection that transcended any dark power Wickham could muster. Our magic surged forward, meeting Wickham's head-on, the collision creating a blinding flash of light.

For a moment, the world seemed to stand still, the two forces locked in a battle of wills. But slowly, inexorably, our magic began to overpower Wickham's, the light pushing back the darkness, driving it away.

Wickham's eyes widened in shock as he realized he was losing, that his dark magic, for all its strength, was no match for the love and unity that fueled our power.

"No!" he screamed, his voice rising in desperation. "This cannot be! I am more powerful than you!"

But it was too late. With a final surge of energy, our magic broke through Wickham's defenses, shattering his dark power and sending him crashing to the ground. The dark tendrils that had once surrounded him dissipated into the air, leaving him weakened and defeated.

He looked up at us, his face twisted in a mixture of fear and disbelief. "You… you cannot win…"

"We already have," I said quietly, my voice tinged with pity. "You lost the moment you chose hate over love."

For a moment, Wickham simply lay there, his once-formidable power reduced to nothing. Then, with a final, despairing cry, he scrambled to his feet and fled into the fog, his figure disappearing into the darkness.

We watched him go, neither of us moving until we were sure he was truly gone. The night was quiet again, the tension that had hung in the air dissipating as the fog began to lift.

Elizabeth turned to me, her eyes filled with both relief and sadness. "It's over, isn't it?"

I nodded, pulling her into my arms. "Yes, it's over. He won't return."

We stood there for a moment, holding each other, the weight of the battle slowly lifting from our shoulders. The town of Longbourn Hollow was finally free from Wickham's malevolent influence, and we could finally begin to build the future we had dreamed of.

As the first light of dawn began to break over the horizon, I looked down at Elizabeth, my heart swelling with love and gratitude. "We did it," I whispered, pressing a kiss to her forehead. "Together."

She smiled, her eyes shining with tears of joy. "Yes, together. And nothing will ever tear us apart again."

We turned back toward Pemberley, the warmth of our home beckoning us forward. The final battle had been fought, and we had emerged victorious— not just over Wickham, but over the doubts, fears, and obstacles that had once stood in our way.

As we walked hand in hand, the sun rising to greet the new day, I knew that this was only the beginning of the life we would build together—a life filled with love, strength, and the unbreakable bond that had brought us to this moment.

And as long as we were together, I knew that we could face anything the future might hold.

20

ELIZABETH

The night before our wedding was meant to be a time of joy and anticipation, but as Darcy and I stood together in the dimly lit drawing room of Pemberley, a sense of foreboding settled over me. The air was thick with the scent of the lavender candles I had lit earlier, their calming fragrance doing little to soothe the unease I felt.

Darcy's hand was warm in mine, his thumb gently stroking the back of my hand as we discussed the final details for the ceremony. "The wards are stronger than ever," he reassured me, his voice a low, comforting rumble. "Pemberley will be protected, as will everyone within its walls."

I nodded, but my mind was elsewhere, distracted by the lingering tension in the air. "It's just nerves, I suppose," I murmured, leaning into him. "But I can't shake the feeling that something is coming."

He kissed the top of my head, his lips lingering against my hair. "We've faced worse, Elizabeth. Together, we're unstoppable."

Before I could respond, a flicker of movement caught my eye. I turned towards the window, the curtains swaying gently as if disturbed by an unseen force. My breath caught in my throat as I saw a figure standing just beyond the boundary of Pemberley's grounds. Even in the shadows, I recognized him immediately—George Wickham.

Darcy stiffened beside me, following my gaze to the man who had caused us so much pain. "He's testing the wards," Darcy said, his voice tense. "But they will hold. He cannot breach them."

I squeezed his hand, drawing strength from his confidence. "What is he doing here, Darcy? Why now?"

He released my hand, his expression hardening as he stepped towards the window. "He's here for revenge, Elizabeth. He's desperate, and he knows this is his last chance to take something from us."

I moved to stand beside him, my heart pounding in my chest. "Then we'll stop him together."

Darcy turned to me, his eyes full of determination and something deeper—fear for my safety. "You'll stay here, Elizabeth. I won't risk you getting hurt."

I shook my head. "No, Darcy. I'm coming with you. My magic is just as strong as yours, and I won't let you face him alone."

For a moment, he looked as if he might argue, but then he nodded, accepting that this was a battle we would fight side by side. "Very well," he said quietly. "But stay close. We don't know what he's capable of."

Together, we stepped out into the night, the cold air biting at our skin as we approached the edge of the wards. Wickham stood just beyond the boundary, his face twisted in a sneer as he watched us approach.

"Darcy, Elizabeth," he greeted us, his voice dripping with mockery. "How touching, the two of you united against a common foe. But you can't stop what's coming."

Darcy's magic flared around him, a protective barrier that shimmered in the darkness. "You won't get past the wards, Wickham. Whatever you're planning, it ends here."

Wickham laughed, a harsh, grating sound that sent a chill down my spine. "You think your wards can stop me? You underestimate how far I'm willing to go."

Without warning, he unleashed a blast of dark magic, the force of it crackling against the wards. The protective barrier held, but I could feel the strain as Wickham's power pressed against it, seeking a weakness.

Darcy stepped forward, his own magic surging to meet Wickham's. "You've already lost, Wickham. Leave now, or face the consequences."

But Wickham was beyond reason. He chanted an incantation, his hands glowing with malevolent energy as he poured everything he had into breaking the wards. The ground beneath us trembled, the air thick with the scent of sulfur and ozone.

I joined my magic with Darcy's, our combined power reinforcing the wards, pushing back against Wickham's assault. Sparks flew around us, the clash of our energies lighting up the night like a storm.

For a moment, it seemed as though we were evenly matched, but then Wickham's magic faltered, his expression twisting with desperation. He pushed harder, but it was clear that he was weakening, his strength no match for the bond that Darcy and I shared.

Seeing his chance, Darcy moved in, his magic

lancing out to seize hold of Wickham's power. With a shout, he drew Wickham's magic into himself, siphoning away the dark energy until Wickham was left gasping and powerless.

"No!" Wickham cried, stumbling back as the last of his magic was ripped away. He fell to his knees, a broken man with nothing left to fight for.

Darcy loomed over him, his voice cold and unforgiving. "You will leave Pemberley and never return. If I ever see you again, Wickham, I won't hesitate to end your life."

Wickham looked up at us, his eyes wide with fear and defeat. "You can't do this," he whispered, but the fight had gone out of him.

"Leave," Darcy commanded, his voice brooking no argument.

Wickham staggered to his feet, casting one last, hate-filled glance at us before turning and disappearing into the night.

As the darkness swallowed him, I let out a breath I hadn't realized I was holding. Darcy turned to me, his face softening as he pulled me into his arms. "It's over," he murmured, his breath warm against my ear. "He's gone."

I wrapped my arms around him, burying my face in his chest. "Tomorrow, we'll be married," I whispered, the weight of the night's events fading as I thought of the future.

Darcy pressed a kiss to my forehead, his hold on me tightening. "I love you, Elizabeth. Forever."

"And I love you," I whispered back, my heart swelling with the certainty that whatever challenges lay ahead, we would face them together.

As we stood there in the moonlit garden, the warmth of Darcy's embrace banishing the lingering chill, I knew that we had won more than just a battle that night. We had secured our future—a future filled with love, magic, and the unbreakable bond that would carry us through whatever came next.

Tomorrow, we would say "I do," and nothing—not even the darkest of forces—could stand in our way.

EPILOGUE

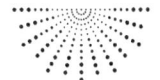

Lydia

The day was perfect, almost too perfect, as if the heavens had decided to grace us with their blessing. I stood on the edge of the garden, just out of sight of the guests, watching as my sister Elizabeth and Mr. Darcy—Fitzwilliam—exchanged their vows under the ancient oak tree at Pemberley. The sunlight streamed through the branches, casting a golden glow over everything, making the scene look like something out of a fairy tale.

I couldn't help but feel a twinge of envy. Not because I wished to be in Lizzy's place—I knew she and Darcy belonged together—but because of the purity of their love, the way they looked at each other as if the rest of the world had melted away. It was the kind of love I had once foolishly thought I had found with Wickham, but now I knew better.

I watched as Darcy leaned down to kiss Elizabeth, his hands cupping her face with such tenderness that it brought a lump to my throat. Elizabeth's eyes fluttered closed, a small, contented smile playing on her lips as she melted into the kiss. The guests erupted in cheers, the sound echoing through the garden, but I remained still, a quiet observer to a moment that felt almost sacred.

As their kiss deepened, something stirred within me—a flicker of hope that perhaps, one day, I too could rebuild my life. Lizzy had promised me that Wickham would never bother me again, and I believed her. Darcy had seen to that, stripping Wickham of his power, leaving him a shadow of the man who had once terrorized me. But even with Wickham gone, the nightmares lingered, creeping into my dreams when I least expected it. The fear that I would never truly be free of his influence haunted me, but I tried to push it aside. Today was about Lizzy and Darcy, about celebrating their love, not dwelling on my past mistakes.

As the ceremony ended, the guests began to disperse, moving toward the reception area where laughter and music awaited. I remained where I was, watching as Lizzy and Darcy walked hand in hand through the garden, their heads close together as they whispered to each other. They were so happy, so in love, and I felt a pang of longing deep in my chest.

"Lydia?"

I turned to see Jane approaching, her soft smile radiating the kind of warmth that only she could offer. She was glowing with happiness, her hand resting gently on her rounded belly—a subtle but unmistakable sign of the love she shared with Charles Bingley.

"Jane," I replied, forcing a smile to my lips. "You look beautiful."

"And you, Lydia," Jane said, her eyes full of concern as she reached out to take my hand. "Are you all right?"

I hesitated, unsure of how to respond. It was so easy to pretend that everything was fine, to put on a brave face and convince the world that I had moved on from the horrors of the past. But Jane knew me too well to be fooled by that.

"I'm trying," I admitted, my voice barely above a whisper. "It's hard, Jane. Sometimes I think I'll never escape what happened."

Jane squeezed my hand, her expression full of empathy. "It will take time, Lydia. But you're stronger than you know. You've already come so far."

I looked into her eyes, the sincerity in her words easing some of the tension that had been coiling inside me. "Do you really think so?"

"I do," Jane said firmly. "And so does Lizzy. We both believe in you, Lydia. You just have to believe in yourself."

I nodded, a small smile tugging at the corners of my lips. Jane's faith in me was unwavering, and for the first time in a long while, I felt a glimmer of that same faith within myself.

"Thank you, Jane," I whispered, my voice thick with emotion. "I don't know what I would do without you and Lizzy."

"You'll never have to find out," Jane replied, her smile widening. "We're always here for you, no matter what."

I wrapped my arms around her, hugging her tightly as the tears I had been holding back finally spilled over. Jane held me close, her presence a comforting balm to the wounds that still lingered just beneath the surface.

As we pulled apart, I caught sight of Lizzy and Darcy again, now surrounded by their guests, who were congratulating them and offering toasts. Lizzy's laughter rang out, light and joyful, and Darcy's eyes never left her, a soft smile playing on his lips as he watched the woman he loved more than anything in the world.

"They're so happy," I murmured, a wistful note in my voice.

"They are," Jane agreed, following my gaze. "And you will be too, Lydia. I know it."

I wanted to believe her, to truly believe that happiness was within my reach. Maybe it wasn't as far away as it seemed.

"Come on," Jane said, linking her arm with mine. "Let's join the others. Today is a day for celebration."

I nodded, allowing her to lead me toward the gathering crowd. As we walked, I couldn't help but glance back at Lizzy and Darcy, their love shining as brightly as the sun overhead. Their journey hadn't been easy, but they had found their way to each other, stronger for all they had endured.

Perhaps, one day, I would find my own path to happiness. It might not be as simple as I once thought it would be, but I was willing to try. And with my family by my side, I knew I wouldn't have to face the journey alone.

As Lizzy and Darcy shared another kiss, their faces alight with the promise of a future filled with love and magic, I felt that flicker of hope grow a little brighter. And maybe, just maybe, that would be enough to build a new life—one that was worthy of the second chance I had been given.

Sign up for Jax Wilder's newsletter and receive a collection of unpublished Coral Cove short stories. Meet familiar characters and dive deeper into the love and romance that Coral Cove is known for. Don't miss out on this exclusive content!

Jax Wilder

If you enjoyed Pride and Prejudice and Witches, I hope you'll check out my **Coral Cove Series,** and my **Tarot Fantasies Series**

The Devil's Temptation

Dottie:

I never believed in fairy tales, but the moment I stepped into The Arcane Room, I felt a magic I'd always denied myself. Ms. Vesper's velvety voice was a spell of its own. She offered me a chance at the forbidden—all I had to do was draw a tarot card. I drew the Devil card. His name was Lucian, His touch was electric, awakening parts of me I'd kept hidden for so long. I wanted to forget every rule I'd ever made for myself and live in this moment forever.

JAX WILDER

Unleash Your Darkest Desires

Dorothea has always played it safe, her life confined to the walls of her bakery in the quaint town of Coral Cove. But when she steps into The Arcane Room, an unassuming new age shop, she's thrust into a world where her deepest fantasies come to life. Guided by the enigmatic and dangerously seductive Lucian, Dottie enters a magical experience where her untouched innocence and hidden passions are brought to the surface.

At twenty-nine, Dottie has never experienced the complexities of intimacy. Her untouched innocence is a stark contrast to Lucian's experienced hands. As he guides her through a series of sensually charged encounters, Dottie learns to confront her fears and embrace the desires she's long kept buried. Lucian's dark allure pushes her boundaries, helping her to uncover her inner strength and face the temptations she has always denied herself.

Within the enchanted simulation, Dottie's journey is one of self-discovery and empowerment. In the heart of The Arcane Room, she learns that true strength comes from within, and living fearlessly is the key to unlocking her greatest desires. Through each tantalizing experience, she discovers the courage to embrace her passions and the power to transform her life.

Will Dottie emerge from the magical realm with the confidence to live her life fully, or will her fears continue to hold her back? Enter a world of seduction, secrets, and self-discovery in "The Devil's Temptation," a spellbinding tale that will leave you breathless and yearning for more.

Discover a story of temptation, transformation, and the power of embracing your true self. "The Devil's Temptation" is an intoxicating journey that will captivate your heart and ignite your imagination.

ALSO BY JAX WILDER

Additional Titles

Coral Cove Series

Sleighed by Love

Harvesting Love

Dawning Desire

Knead You Now

Love Rewound

Haunted by Her

Perfect Lover Spell

Tarot Fantasies Series

The Devil's Temptations

Strength of the Beast

Hanged Passions

Death's Embrace

6 of Cups

3 of Swords

Jax Wilder

Additional Books by

Rainbow Quartz Publishing

Lorelai Hamilton

Find Your Bliss

Teenage Witch's Grimoire

Tarot Reflection Journal

Tarot Refection Journal Coloring The Tarot

The Eclectic Witch's Grimoire

Dream Journal

Teenage Tarot

Tarot Tales and Magic Spells

Arcane In Verse

Miranda Levi

From A Youth A Fountain Did Flow

The Sea Withdrew

A Tear In Time

Mo(ther) Na(ture)

In Orion's Hands

Jackson Anhalt

From The 911 Files

Isla Watts

A Fairy Bad Day

Surprise! You're a Vampire

Gorgeous, Gorgeous, Gorgons

Mork The Handsome Orc

Adopted By Werewolves

Bite Me If You Can

That's The Spirit!

Rose Dawson's Book Journals

My Time With The Fairies

Enchanted Escapades

Enchanted Escapades

Dewey Decimal Diaries

Siren's Songbook

Pride and Prejudice

Bibliophile's Bounty

Book of Books Journal

Pages & Passages Reading Journal

Bookworm's Companion Reading Journal & Tracker

ABOUT THE AUTHOR

Jax Wilder is a passionate romance author hailing from a charming small town nestled in the picturesque Pacific Northwest. With a heart full of love and an unyielding belief in the power of happily ever afters, Jax weaves enchanting tales of love and connection that leave readers captivated.

Jax's novels are a reflection of her commitment to celebrating the magic of love, and her characters' journeys mirror the warmth and happiness she has found in her own life. Join her on the enchanting journey of love, passion, and enduring connection through her heartfelt romance novels.

www.ingramcontent.com/pod-product-compliance
Lightning Source LLC
Chambersburg PA
CBHW061218170626

46809CB00007B/2518